MW00768275

CHIRON review

ISSUE #119, FALL 2020

ST. JOHN, KANSAS

CHIRON review

Issue #119, fall 2020

Poetry Editors
Wendy Rainey, Clint Margrave
Kareem Tayyar, Grant Hier

Fiction Editors
Rafael Zepeda, Sarah Daugherty

Art /Design: Craig Ashby

Cover art: #piggybanksy

Chiron Review is indexed by *Humanities International Complete*. Issues 18-81 were indexed by *Index of American Periodical of Verse*. *CR* is microfilmed by ProQuest, Ann Arbor, MI, and its archive is housed at Beinecke Rare Book & Manuscript Library, Yale U., New Haven, CT.

Opinions expressed by the writers and artists in this journal are their own and not to be considered those of the publisher or the editors.

ISSN: 1046-8897

ISBN: 978-0-943795-98-0

Michael Hathaway, Publisher
chironreview2@gmail.com / www.chironreview.com
Additional copies of this issue also available at Lulu.com

Donations to Chiron, Inc. are welcome via Paypal with our email address, editor@-chironreview.com, check, or money order.

❧ Contents ❧

4

dear landlord,

yes, those were squad cars
on the street last night,
again
but they were here for that
malcontent next door pounding on the walls
shouting demands of the universe

while naked, then rolling around in the

yard screaming like a rabbit in a fox's
jaw after I gave him one pint glass
of wine, and refused to let him
use my phone,

I did not know,

believe me.

dear landlord,

that piney, citrus
smell
emanating from the kitchen
cupboard isn't cat-piss

and it wasn't my cat.

J. Lester Allen

dear landlord,

yes, that was me in my
underwear early this morning educating
the college kids upstairs
on neighborly etiquette after
them deciding that 1:30 am on a Tuesday
is prime time for an acoustic
Bruce Springsteen
singalong, no offense to
The Boss.

J. Lester Allen

Abuela's Face

Ximena is twelve when her *tia*
phones to say it's time to come
to the funeral parlor to put make-up
on her Grandma's inert face, a request
her *abuela* made a few months ago,
Please, Ximena, you put the make-up
on my face when I die; the funeral
directors make a woman look
like a whore.

She goes to Grandma's house as quickly
as a pubescent girl can with dignity
and searches in Grandma's dressing
table drawer for base, blush, eyebrow
pencil, eye-liner, eye shadow, mascara
and the subdued pink lipstick she knows
Grandma keeps there.

At the funeral home, Grandma's skin
is leathery when Ximena holds her chin
securely as she smooths the base
across her Grandma's forehead
and tints her cheeks with blush.

The funeral director has closed
Grandma's eyes leaving pesos
on the eyelids to keep them secured,
so outlining them with eye-liner
and brushing mascara on Grandma's
eye-lashes is easier than she thought
it would be. Grandma's lipstick,
sticky to apply, looks natural
with just a little gloss.

Okay, Grandma, ready for viewing,
Ximena thinks, and smiles as she
kisses her *abuela's* cold hands.

Jan Ball

Evolution's copy editor

misses the occasional
typo, allows the bot fly,
the deer tick, the oak
mite to sneak by –
perhaps to test
our attention span –

keeps us awake
bragging how
he slipped *Trypanosoma*
past our sleepily
nodding heads,

then, to relieve
the boredom, watches
our reaction
to the question mark
of the hookworm.

Roy Beckemeyer

The Beginning

Make me take it back: the past domestic grift.
Say, *Rewind like a film reel. You don't*
want to miss the scene with the fire.
I know it's symbolic of your father,
an alcoholic – bitter, brutal, lost – &
I'm an addict, which means nothing good
between us. & would I reverse it? I doubt
that solves anything. We were ignoring
each other long before my wrongs,
or yours. How far would we have to twist
the celluloid back? To the opening credits?
Or the first act where a scared man runs
down an alley, his face shadowed
as though an eagle flies above him?
We don't know who's chasing him,
or whom he's after, one way or the other.

Ace Boggess

thunder alley

for kell robertson and john dorsey

wearing clean jeans
on the road is a luxury
today is all luxury

turkey vultures circle overhead
they smell the fox news
we picked up in a central
missouri bowling alley

dorsey and I
read kell robertson
in the driveway
under the osage sun

we are poets
out of place
noises in the dark
our disasters are voluntary

Jason Baldinger

Earth Day

But first, Earth Night – its tempest,
    percussive nails of fire.

Its torrent. Morning finally limping
    through the gray curtain, shell-shocked,

dripping. The ground gasping
    and sloshing into boots.

Against the tree line, a tiny fawn galloping
    behind one hardly older.

A single tom circling the field in jerky
    pantomime, displaying to himself.

And the creek, oh my.
    Last winter, parched bed we followed

the crooks of, you and I, for miles
    over dry rock, puddles of small bloated fish

until a barbed fence halted us.
    Now, a churning monster of whitewater

and hurtled debris. Wave upon
    wave seizing the banks.

Back at your place, stick of dogwood
    that survived the drought,

the sun's hot hand on your neck,
    everywhere a tumult of green.

The *chuck chuck* of a red-bellied woodpecker,
    hidden in uncurling canopy,

leading you from tree to tree
    on a fool's errand, your favorite kind.

You'd forgotten the day was official –
    later postings would remind,

the pleas for help to oppose
    and to preserve. You, I couldn't help.

But those deer reminded me that today
    I had pledged to walk the road,

pledged to the ghost
    of a slain young buck to rescue

its skull from the buzzards' final pickings,
    shake last maggots from splintered

nostrils, bleach it white, the nubs
    of horn all they would ever be.

Gaylord Brewer

On This Day, 1960

Of course, it fascinates
that seven times the number of women
today complete college
as opposed to before the approval
for sale of Enovid-10
(first medicine ever
designed for those who weren't ill).
And the effect of that small circular case
on the history of sexual mores
and feminist ideology truly astounds.

The Pill's cultural earthquake, however,
somehow doesn't measure
to the ancient Egyptians' paste of crocodile dung
as pessary (a rare word
for which none other suffices). Meanwhile,
archeologists hotly debate the condom's
existence as early as 3000 BC,
popularly made of fish bladders,
perhaps. Antonius Liberalis, however,
related in 150 AD that the ever-considerate
Minos, his semen a tempest
of serpents and scorpions, preferred
the sturdy goat bladder as protection.

There remains the contested
original use of the loincloth, while the Chinese
upper-classes of the 15th century committed
to encapsulations of oiled silk paper
or lamb intestine. While in Japan,
reportedly … well, let us not dwell on that,
nor on the Middle Ages' innovations
of covering the penis in tar or a soak
of onion juice.

Centuries later, Casanova claimed a simple
half lemon as cervical cap did the trick,
resolving the matter.

So, cheers to family-planning pioneer
Margaret Sanger, the chemistry of Carl Djerassi,
temerity of the FDA and the greed
of Big Pharmaceutical. Cheers to all
theorists and practitioners of yore.
Hi-ho to gender rights, sexual freedom
and a well-earned diploma.

I will tell you, though, we have wasted
much time and exertion. My wife
(a highly educated woman, please note),
angrily in the next room
and unspeaking to me since last night,
offers a response to the subject at hand
practical and profound.
A timeless solution to our worries.

Gaylord Brewer

Rachel Bullock

Body Count

I start sleeping with my therapist during our second appointment. Her name is Theodora Elizabeth Zitkus. Theo for short. She kisses me after seeing her name in my notebook. I keep a running list of all the people I have ever loved or considered loving. Sixty or so names all color coordinated. The colors distinguish the levels of intimacy. Names in blue meant penetrative sex. Names in purple meant kissing. Names in red meant sex without penetration. Names in black meant nothing physical transpired. In retrospect the color choices were not my best. Theo says, the list looks like a fresh bruise, then she sees her own name written in pencil at the end – pencil for in progress.

My roommate Emily is not into it. When I get home from my appointment her head pops up from behind the couch. The worn red leather backing, blocks her out so she's just a floating head of black hair.

"How was it?" she asks.

"I fucked my therapist."

"Funny."

"I'm serious."

Her arm moves up to the back of the couch, and she pushes herself up so she's now, a head, a shoulder and a forearm. Some black hair escapes the stumpy ponytail at the back of her head. A slightly greasy strand sticks to her cheek. She blows it of her face with a huff. Her eyes skim my existence. My heart is racing and for brief moment her cool veil drops, and the wheels turning in her head can be heard throughout our apartments small living room. Then she's back, cold stone.

"Okay well congratulations I guess."

I hang on the tinge of irritation in her voice.

The sex happens like this:

"So," Theo says at our first appointment, "you can't stop wondering what your own skin tastes like?" She's reading off a print out of my entrance interview.

"Uh yeah," I say, "I've tried banana peels, walnuts, the little strip of rubbery glue that holds together notepads." I tap my pointer finger and thumb together as if that's the universal mime for such things.

"Hmmm."

16

The inside of her office is trying too hard to be inoffensive. Some-one's painted the walls a yellowy-beige, and picked saw dust for carpet color, and she only has two pictures hanging up: a painting of white daffodils, and a picture of a cat that looks disturbingly sad.

"None of them taste like me."

"And does this surprise you?" Her words hold no inflection. She's deadpan. Devoid of judgement, which is somehow more unnerving.

"Not really."

I wait for her to ask me another question. She waits too. Her eyes are moss colored and they peel me like an onion. I'm glad I wore clean underwear. We sit in silence for a full minute. She keeps a clock on the end table beside her. One with a big round face, and a second hand tick, that sounds a little off. Like every-other second comes too quickly. She uncrosses her legs and re-crosses them.

I can hear someone outside her office window. Their feet slapping against the pavement drown out the clock. The same person walking by is loudly singing *there was a time when men were kind,* from a Broad-way show that sounds familiar but I can't remember the name of.

"That feels objectively untrue," I say nodding my head towards the window.

Theo's face is open and blank, but she says nothing. She uncrosses her leg and re-crosses. She's mirroring me. Trying to make me feel comfortable. That or she loves me. People mimic the people they want to fuck for some reason.

I've done it. When I first realized I liked women I did research. The internet had a lot to say about lesbians. Short nails came up more than once, so, my nails kept getting shorter and shorter and shorter until my nailbeds were bloody. If I met a woman who I thought might be inter-ested in me, I'd keep moving my hands to her line of vision as if to say, *look! look! I'm like you.*

"So, why don't we talk about," Theo scans the print out again, "your mother."

I bring my body count in the next week so that we don't have to talk about my mother. Then we don't end up talking at all. Theo makes love to me delicately. Her lips trail down my neck, and circle my nipple, and her tongue scoops into my belly button. Her hands consistently run across my chest, not my breasts, but my sternum, as if she's checking for a heartbeat. It must be the doctor in her. She grinds her hips into me so hard that the rug on her office floor eats a fresh rash of rug burn into my tailbone. It's sort of a pleasant sting. The kind of pain that reminds you you're alive.

17

"It looks like tire tracks," Emily says later that night. She's sitting in the tub with the water on. I'm examining myself in the mirror that the last tenants drilled into the bathroom wall. "Or maybe like bed bug bites."

Emily has her hair pulled to the top of her head, but it's too short, so she has an array of bobby pins along the back of her neck, keeping her hair from the tub water. She pulls one of the pins out and throws it at me.

"Water's getting cold," she says. Emily likes things like herbal bath, and dried flowers that keep negative energy away. Every cup in our apartment is a recycled jam, or sauce jar. She think's mint leave oil keeps insects and mice out of our cupboards. She has no problem getting naked in front of people, especially me. Bathing together somehow became our weekly tradition.

I twist in the mirror so I can see my back one last time, and then get into the tub across from her. The water stings the raw skin, and I let out a pained hiss. Emily pulls her knees to her chest to give me more room. Our toenails scrape, as I get comfortable.

"No offense but this bubble bath smells like it's going to give me a yeast infection."

"It's just essential oils," and after a clipped pause she adds, "I think I met someone too."

"I hope the word yeast infection didn't remind you of him."

She swats bath water at me, and soapy water sloshes over the lip of the tub. I knew she met someone weeks ago. I heard her whispering in her room with a sort of manic, hormonal high schooler tone to her voice. A tone she reserved for boyfriends, and doctor's office secretaries.

"What's he look like?" I ask.

"*She,*" she says, "kind of looks like that one girl that was on *LA Bachelor*, the blond one."

"They're all blond."

"I think her name was Becca."

"The real thin one who still managed to have a double chin and look like a parakeet?" I can only vaguely remember the faces of the contestants. I hardly watched the show. I just happened to be on the couch while it played.

She nods her head.

"So, you like women now?" I blurt.

She shrugs, "I don't like all women –"

"Well neither do I."

"She's just different, I guess. I don't know."

18

She runs her hands over the top of the water and some of the foam from the tub mixture clings to the palm of her hand. She keeps her touch light as to not break the surface tension.

"Cool," I say finally, "That's really cool."

When we get out of the tub, she grabs my shoulders before I can leave the bathroom.

"Let me put some aloe on your back," she says. She pulls at the towel under my arms, and it falls to the floor. The coolness of the aloe makes me jump, and I turn. We collide a little and both laugh. "Come on," she says, turning me back away from her, "This will help it heal."

"Why don't you tell me about some of your part relationships?" Theo asks. It's the third week, and our third appointment together. It's strange that she still wants to play the therapy game. How can she take my words seriously when my mouth has been on and around her labia? I'm bored. I sink down into the overstuffed chair, and let my cheek fall against the soft leather.

"That might take a while."

I peek up at her. She looks ethereal. Her long auburn hair is pulled back with a banana clip, highlighting the sharpness of her jawline. Her lips are slightly chapped, and swollen from kissing me. She repeats the question when I don't answer. I realize she might be asking for selfish reasons.

"Well, I don't think I've ever had a relationship," I say finally.

Her therapist mask slips off for a second. "The book?"

"That's sex, and love, not relationships, that's different."

She writes something on her notepad. I learn forward to see what it says, and she tilts the pad of paper up, and towards her chest. She gives me a teasing smile.

"Why don't you tell me about a memory that stands out to you?" she asks.

I tell her about Max from high school. The first name on the list.

Max and I both worked at an ice cream shop part-time after school. We flirted relentlessly for two months before he finally invited me to his house. My virginity felt like wearing a heavy coat during the hottest day in August. I liked him enough. He stuck enamel pins into his snap-back, and played the piano in a band with forty-year-old white men. And he liked me. All I could remember from his house was that I pocketed the grocery list stuck to the fridge, and I considered the bananas sitting on the counter, browned almost to the point of rotting.

He was the first person I ever saw naked. Apart from my father on accident or underwear models, or crude sketches in high school textbooks. He came out of the showers as I was climbing the stairs of his empty house. He had a trail of dark hair climbing the slope of his stomach. He swung his cock around and I, still on the second landing of his stairs, was right at eye level. Later her would weave his fingers through mine. And I'd think about how my mother once pressed our hands into two c's that met in the middle, and said *this handhold is for mommy, this,* she laced our fingers together like shoe laces, *is for your husband.*

I didn't have sex with him. We touched each other clumsily. Awkwardly. He put his hand in my pants, but used my underwear as a barrier. I didn't come. He said, *you have the biggest boobs out of any girl I've been with.* I said, *Thanks.* How many girls had there been? Him, younger than me, eighteen to my nineteen. I felt less-than. Behind. I had only kissed one, maybe two guys, and a handful of my girl friends at middle school sleepovers. *Have you done ... it?* He asked. *It.* Such a small word. I could lie. *Of course.* Then he came, but I worried I didn't make it happen fast enough. I wasn't worried he'd tell his friends I was easy, rather that I gave defective blow jobs.

"And that's why I'm a gay," I joke when I finish telling the story to Theo. She doesn't laugh. She's still furiously transcribing my words onto her notepad. "I'm only joking. That's not how it works." I sound stupid.

"I'm really sorry that happened to you," she says when she's done writing.

I let her finish writing and then ask, "Want to come back to my place when the hour's up?"

I bring Theo back to Emily and I's shithole two-bedroom. She leaves her office fifteen minutes after me, and parks around the block from my building. I run into the apartment before her and throw all the half-filled water jars in the sink, and straighten the stack of poetry books Emily keeps by the coffee table.

"Hey! Hey!" I call into the apartment. Emily's door is slightly ajar and her room is dark. She's not home, and I'm slightly disappointed. Theo knocks on the door, a few minutes later. She's taken off the blazer she had on in the office, and has untucked the slip-style shirt from her trousers. Her shoulders are bare and freckled, and her hair is hanging down her back, slightly kinked from having it pulled up in a clip. I hold open the door and motion for her to come in.

"Want some wine?"

20

"Just a small glass," she says. She holds her purse in front of her, and follows me into the kitchen. I can feel her behind me, shifting her weight between her kitten heals.

"Go sit down, and relax," I say. I hear her click out of the kitchen, and the sigh of the couch in the living room as she sits. I pour the wine into two jars, that once held the green olives Emily likes.

Theo's sitting on the couch, touching the collectables I keep on the coffee table. She's fingering a plum sized ceramic elephant, painted to look jade. She holds it up to me as I set the wine down in front of her.

"This is nice," she says. I took it from a man named Jim, or John, or maybe even Jacob. He said it came from a temple in India. A forgotten sticker on the bottom suggested an airport gift shop. He didn't even realize it was gone.

"It was my grandmother's," I say, "she had a thing for elephants, collected them. It's real jade."

I wait for Theo to catch me in my lie. It seems like something a therapist might do, but she only makes satisfied noise, and sets the elephant back on the table.

We drink wine and fool around on the couch. As I kiss Theo's neck, she makes the same *hmm* sounds, she makes during our sessions. I move from her neck to her lips, and the sounds continue. Her lips are vibrating against my teeth. Then I realize it's her phone vibrating in her purse. She tumbles off me, and the couch, covering her exposed breast as if someone has just walked in. I look up and over the couch to see if Emily actually has come.

"Hello," she answers the phone in a chipper voice, "Oh hi honey, uh yeah, I just had a client who needed me a little later. I'm on my way home now."

"Am I the other woman?" I ask when she hangs up. I'm trying out her therapy voice. I'm not offended, just asking a question. She blinks at me, and holds the phone to her chest. I think she might start crying. "I'm cool with that," I say. She relaxes a little but her bottom lip is quivering.

I sit up on the couch, and pull my shirt back down over my bare stomach. I kiss the top of her head because I don't have the answers.

Emily brings her new flame home two weeks later. She's bird-boned, and has a slender pixy like nose, and aggressively long eyelashes. She blinks and I feel like I'm getting blown backwards. Her mouth disproportionately consumes her face. Kind of like a lizard. I don't know how Emily kisses her.

"This is my roommate HJ," Emily says, "She's my best friend from college. We met freshman year and have been stuck at the hip since," Emily grabs the other girl's hand, and they share a secret smile, "and HJ this is Leah."

The impulse to bolt from the apartment crawls over my skin. I stay put. Extend my hand to shake Leah's but, she still has her hand in Emily's.

"You have something on your sock," is all Leah says to me, and she points to a piece of glitter washy-tape matted to my big toe.

"Nice to meet you too."

I turn on the radio in my room, and listen to the static-filled station on max volume. I organize the things on my bookshelf. I have a system. The bottom shelf is, receipts, grocery lists, and some pocket lint. And other miscellaneous small things like a few plastic tooth flossers, and a stack of stock-paper cards. Some are appointment reminders and others are just business related. The middle shelf is heavier things. A dish of spare change. A package of staple refills. And an assortment of polished rocks, and minerals. I have a few figurines too. A cow dressed as a librarian, and small nondescript blob carved into a smiling face – something one of my past partners made out of modeling clay. The top shelf has more mis-matched things. My favorite though is a photo taken from a Trevor on my list. It's a half-developed Polaroid picture. Just a smudge of flesh, and blond hair. There's something particularly haunting about it. Even though I didn't really like Trevor, I bought a small frame for it and everything.

I call Theo using the emergency number on her website. She answers on the second ring and her voice breaks a little when I say my name.

"I'm having some intrusive thoughts," I say. I hear her voice, distant from the phone, maybe talking to her husband. Then footsteps, and then a door closing.

"I just moved into the laundry room," her voice is low and breathy, "Do you need me to come to you?"

A fluttery laugh breaks through the music playing in my room. It's not Emily. I've never hated the sound of laughter more. The dial on the radio won't turn left any further.

"I want to talk about my book," I say. I'm sitting on my bedroom floor, behind my bed, with the book spread over my crossed legs. My thumb glides over Theo's name in pencil. I've been meaning to re-write it in red ink, but it's normally something I do once the relationship has ended.

"I'm having a hard time hearing you," she says. I repeat myself a few times and when she still can't hear me, I reluctantly turn down my radio. When I repeat, *I want to talk about my book,* my voice comes out too loud, and the sound of it makes me cringe. I look back towards my bedroom door. Emily has music playing in her room too. I don't hear any talking.

I blindly pick a name from my list.

"I want to talk about Carmen."

I hear moving on the other end of the phone. I wonder if Theo can sense my position through my voice, and is now sitting cross-legged on her laundry room floor – like she might in her office.

"Okay, what's so memorable about Carmen in particular?"

I tell her:

The summer of my sophomore year of college, my mother rented a beach house on the coast of Maine. I got a part-time job at a local A&P, mostly to have an excuse to leave the house. Carmen was my shift manager, and coincidentally we finally fucked the week Emily came to stay with me. Carmen invited us to a house party. Emily didn't want to go. She hated parties, but she encouraged me to go, *get your girl,* she kept saying.

Carmen wore a Hawaiian shirt, completely unbuttoned. Her stomach and breasts were partially exposed. She moved slightly, and the flowered fabric pulled from her skin. She had duct-tape printed with little dogs covering her nipples. She also carried a pocket knife. I could feel it in her jean pocket as we rubbed up against each other in the house's dining room.

The smell of artificial bananas had permanently soaked into her skin from a summer of wearing sunscreen. She used her fingers to make me orgasm. After I came, I felt empty. Like it expelled me from my body. Hollowed me out. I started crying, and she sat up, repeating, *oh my god, did I hurt you? Did I hurt you?*

I feel like might cry now on the phone with Theo but I swallow the urge.

"If I could come over right now, I'd make you come." She's whispering so softly I almost can't hear her over the music seeping out of Emily's room. I pull the phone away from my ear and look at it, and after a moment bring it back to my head, and give a lukewarm *yeah?*

The letter comes without warning. It's written on yellow paper with blue lines, and after staring at it I realize it's from Theo's notepad. It says a lot of things in her curly black handwriting, but the most alarming is:

I'm reduced to a thing that wants Harper.

I show the letter to Emily when Leah's not over.

"Wow," she says. She flattens the paper against coffee table and re-reads it a few more times. "The reduced thing is a Virginia Woolf quote. Something she wrote to her lover."

"Like *Who's Afraid of Virginia Woolf?*"

"She didn't write that," Emily says. She folds the letter into a paper airplane, and throws it to where I lay on the couch. The tip of the plane collides with my thigh, and falls to the floor.

"Are you in love?" she asks after a breath.

I shrug. She doesn't really react. She just stares at me, or through me, sometimes I can't tell. I wonder if she thinks Theo is the first person to ever love me. I've thought about showing her my body count before, letting her pour over the names in different colors, but that feels to overt, like showing her the book would be the same as screaming: *Hey look someone wanted to fuck me. I'm worthy.*

"Why?" I ask.

"Why what?" She's not paying attention to me anymore. She's smiling at her cellphone. I think about slamming a throw pillow into her face but I can't move. A thin line of sweat has me stuck to the leather couch.

"Why did you ask me, if I'm in love?"

She shrugs now. Does she want me to ask her if she's in love with Leah? Sometimes people only ask questions so they can find an entry way into talking about themselves. She's done it to me before.

One night during sophomore year, she rolled out of her twin bed, and climbed in next to me. She had just broken up with her high school boyfriend of three years. Her first love. I thought she had cried herself into a deep sleep.

You awake? she asked. Her breath stuck to the side of my face. She pressed her forehead into the side of my head. I nodded my head yes. *Can I sleep here?* I nodded again.

We were silent for a while.

Do you believe anyone can make it last?

Huh?

Like do you think humans are meant to be monogamous?

Her boyfriend had cheated on her. I had to say the right thing. I rolled over so that my nose touched the end of hers. She giggled a little, when our skin brushed. Her breath traced the lines of my lips.

I think when the right people find each other, yes. Do you?

She had swollen eyelids, and her irises looked darker, maybe from

24

excessive crying. She nodded her head a little, and her nose brushed up and down against mine. Her eyes fluttered. I realized she was already drifting into sleep. I kissed her gently on the mouth. If she felt it, she didn't react. We slept in my bed every night for a week. Then she met Caleb.

At my next appointment I don't bring up the letter, but Theo kisses me as soon the door closes. She tries to deepen the kiss and I turn my head, giving her the side of my mouth. I sit her in her desk chair and go down on her. As she's about to climax, she whimpers, "I think I'm going to leave my husband." I make eye contact with the cat picture on the wall behind her head. I've never seen anything more heinous.

I sit back on my knees, and look up at her. Her skin's flushed, and the hair on the right side of her head is coming out of her ponytail. She's panting a little.

"Are you going to say anything?" she asks.

"That letter was kind of a lot," I say. Then my whole-body hiccups, and I don't realize I've left her sitting naked from the waist down in her office chair until I'm standing in the middle of the parking lot.

When I get home, Emily is in the kitchen cooking. She has on clothes from my closet. I recognize the sweat pants, and the button down. I don't say anything to her. I just lean against the counter, and try to space out. She jumps when she notices me.

"Fuck me," she says, "Are you trying to put me in the ground early?"

I try to tell her about Theo, but the opportunity seems to come and go quickly. The water in the pot is boiling over, and she has her back to me again, tending to the pasta. She turns the flame down.

"Leah's coming over for dinner," she says, then pauses to look at me, "Just so you know."

I mull it over. "Are you trying to ask me to leave the apartment without saying it?"

She's stirring the pasta with a wooden spoon, and when she turns to look at me, she brings it to her hip, and her eyebrows go all the way up to her hair line.

"Why are you so grumpy?"

"I'm not," I say, but my voice betrays me. She sets the spoon on the counter, and walks towards me. She doesn't have makeup on. Her hair's unwashed, and she's wearing my sweatpants. "You going to change for your big date?" She looks down at herself.

25

"No," she says. Confusion contorts her face. My stomach drops. It's more offensive than if she had on heels and hoop earrings. She's already comfortable enough to be herself in front of Leah.

"Well maybe you should."

"Damn," she says, "Okay, you don't need to be a bitch."

I want to obliterate her. To make her feel like nothing.

She is nothing. She is nothing. She is nothing.

I don't even realize I'm saying it out loud until Emily reacts.

"Who are you talking about?" she asks.

I hide in my bedroom for the rest of the night. Not that I need too, Emily takes the pasta, and Leah into her bedroom and closes the door. Around 11:30 p.m. Theo knocks on our apartment door. She has a rim of clumpy mascara under her eyes. When I open the door, she hurls herself into me.

"I got in a fight with Michael," she says as she walks in. She sets her purse on the floor, and is starting to take off her jacket.

"What happened?" I ask. She's made her way into the living room and has laid her jacket over the back of the couch. I'm still standing with my hand on the door, holding it open. I can hear that the music is lower in Emily's room. Can she hear us?

She lets out a noise caught between a sigh and a growl, and pushes her hair back into her skull. She stares at the stucco-ceiling. "He's just a miserable, asshole."

I don't say anything, because what can I say to that.

"Can I stay here tonight?"

Her eyes go from the ceiling to my face to the door still open in my hand.

"Tonight, isn't really good for me."

We stare at each other. "Sorry," I add. She folds her coat over her forearm and walks back around the couch. She picks up her purse and stands in front of me.

"What am I to you?" she asks.

"Well," I start but then I realize I don't have an answer, which in some ways in an answer. The tears pour from her again. She has her head in her hands, and she's saying things but it's like she trying to talk to me from underwater. I know it's the wrong thing to do, but as soon as she's in the hallway I shut the door. She must hear the lock click.

She knocks again.

"Harper," she says, "Harper. I'm still out here."

I take a step back from the door, and then another, until I run into the back of the couch, and startle myself. "You're sick," she says, "You

26

can't just use people out of boredom and loneliness."

I call for Emily, but Leah's comes out of her room. She doesn't have pants on, and I can see the slope of her bare breasts under her flannel shirt. Well, my flannel shirt I realize. The one Emily had on earlier.

Emily stumbles out behind her. She's bare-legged, in a shirt that's also mine. She has a line of drool crusted to her chin from sleep.

"What's going on?" She rubs at her eyes. I hear her but the words don't really process. I can only see the brown, olive stripes of my shirt hanging over Leah's thin shoulders.

"You better let me in," Theo shouts from the hallway. She must be using both hands to hit the door. "You can't just leave me out here."

I grab at the sleeve covering Leah's arm the way a lover might. Leah freezes. All three of us pause momentarily. Theo's voice comes through the door.

"Caleb. Andrew. Lidia. Kate. Jacqulyn. Matt. Morgen." The names bounce around the apartment, around us, standing there, my hand on Leah's sleeve, Emily's hand hovering around my shoulder. "Are they in there with you now Harper? Huh? Are they? Are they? Where are they now? Shelby. Connor. Alex. Anna. Courtney. Emily."

I know the Emily Theo's screaming about is not my Emily, but still the name sends a shudder down my spine.

"What the fuck is going on?" Leah asks. Her question triggers me. Who is she to ask such a question? I yank on the sleeve of her shirt – my shirt really – like I'm yanking a wax strip from skin covered in hair. She yelps as if I've hurt her. The buttons closing the flannel over her ribcage, pop free, and fall to the floor.

I stumble back, not because I want to but because Emily has me by the arm and the shoulder, and is moving me. Leah has her hands to her throat, holding the ripped collar – suddenly modest. There is a brief pause of silence, besides Theo's incessant knocking. Her voice still calling out names that don't belong to anyone inside the apartment. We all stare at the buttons on the apartment floor.

Emily lets go of me and I lunge for the buttons. Emily follows. Leah screeches. They both think I'm going after Leah's feet. Leah scrambles back into Emily's room and slams the door shut. Emily sits on the small of my back, pushing all her weight into me. I'm basically doing the breast stroke against hardwood. My fingers wrap around a button just as she turns me over.

I swat at her. I connect with strands of hair, a shoulder, but not the mass of her.

"Get off of me," I say. "Get off." I'm still swatting. She catches one of my flailing arms and pins it to the floor against my body.

27

"What …" her voice is disjointed from trying to pin me down, "is wrong with you?"

"I don't want you –" I say, "Get off of me. You're crushing me. You're crushing me."

"What are you talking about?" Her voice is strained. Leah is whimpering in the bedroom. Every few breathes I hear her nasally voice calling, "Is everything okay?"

All at once Emily stops trying to grab my other arm, and folds. Her hands collapse against my chest, and she leans forward. Her hair skims the edge of my face. Tears or maybe snot – I realize she's sobbing so hard it's all mixed together –drips onto my cheek. I stop moving under her. She's crying. I don't say anything, because I don't know what to say. I don't want to say the wrong thing. I don't want her to shut off, and leave me again. To stop myself from talking I put the button from my hand into my mouth. I grind it between my teeth. The button tastes briefly of salt, then sweet almost, but doesn't melt like candy, it's just plastic and nothing.

Another tear falls from Emily's eyes onto my cheek. It's warm, and I feel it roll all the way down the side of my face, and pool in the canal of my ear. I can still hear Theo in the hallway. Or maybe it's Leah. Or Emily. It's hard to hear anything over Emily. She's all of us. We're all crying. Our fists in time against the wooden door. The entire inside of our apartment thrumming, something like a heartbeat.

Last Cast at Valley Forge

We crossed the creek under Mt. Joy
where Lafayette marched bootless
farmers carrying sticks for muskets
because the army couldn't afford muskets
or even soldiers to carry them into war,
but that's old history, and this creek now
gives its stories up with difficulty,
so Scott tied on a blue-winged olive
barely the size of a dust spider,
cast it past a tree root and hooked
a small trout desperate enough to risk
an open display of hunger, and then
Scott tells me his wife is sick, not
coming home and he'd already planned
to take the family back west after,
where folks are waiting to take the part
of mother. Did you know, he says, Quakers
abandoned their farms here when
the army came because they wanted
no part of that fight, Washington
turned the forge to making cannon balls,
and all the farms turned to mud.
We fished up to the dam, walked
the horse path a mile to another bend
until the sun lay down behind Mt. Misery.
What do you do, he said, when life
throws this at you? We followed
the growing shadows along the creek,
each candlelit leaf leading back
to the beginning, our waders heavy
on our legs with water, the season
over, the moon ready to take its turn.

Grant Clauser

Peacock Hill

What if we give up on forgiveness and instead
    walk through the brambles to the top of the rise
        and watch the wild peacocks roost in the trees.

Turquoise and emerald, fringed and crested cobalt –
    let's soak our eyes in color and kneel in the dirt, tune
        ourselves with the infrasonic music of their wings.

We've been too long splintered and bandaged.
    Who bought that ax we shoulder between us,
        those scales that weigh our sins like the city measures

garbage hauled from office parks?
    If you need to find my weakness, I'll lay it out before you
        and write its story in blood. I don't think you'll be surprised

by the dozen eyes, the luster of plum and gold.
    I am, after all, a figment of what you think I am.
        What if we climb the trees and lie in the canopy of night

and whisper our secrets to the peahens.
    They know enough of love to give us good advice.
        Look how patiently they sit on their nest of eggs

while coyotes sneer beyond the field of feathers.
    Hold an egg in your hand and paint our resurrection.
        No matter what you think about our chances,

let morning find us iridescent and shimmering.

Sandy Coomer

Seven Ways of Looking at a Shooting

1. Circle, circle, pool of molten lava
   congealed at the rim, the scent of metal,
   smoke, a piece of wood smoldering.
2. Stick figure drawn on paper, an outline
   of a sentence, the modifiers dangling like legs.
3. A phone call, a family, blue lights, white lights,
   a flashing yellow, an echo, a morning of ash.
4. What do we do with this city when a man
   can't walk in his own neighborhood,
   when a man can't walk, when a man can't.
5. Statistics and numbers and counting.
   Someone in city hall knows the percentages,
   equations, multiplication, square roots
   and subtraction, subtraction.
6. Morgue-cold, metal trays, a face beneath
   a sheet, a toe tag, a funeral home, a grave.
7. Question: Can you blame him? Yes.
   Question: Can you blame him? No.
   We turn circles. We speak lava.
   We start over from the beginning.

Sandy Coomer

Gray baby blues

Bye-bye dye,
women sure do mystify,
they got this urge to beautify,
bye-bye dye, goodbye.

Bye-bye dye,
women can be so sly,
I didn't know that colors lie,
bye-bye dye, goodbye.

Oh, momma, the gray's here to stay,
now don't you hide yourself away.

Bye-bye, dye,
my gal's hair pleased my eye,
always sparkled like the sky,
bye-bye dye, goodbye.

Bye-bye dye,
those sweet tresses made me sigh
made me sweat like July,
bye-bye dye, goodbye.

Oh, pretty baby all I got to say
is your blue eyes hide the gray.

Eric Chiles

Clam Bangle

I reckon you read
The ebbs and flows
Like the back of your hand,
Went clam hunting regularly
And had a knack for fashioning
Bangles and an array of
Clam accessories way before
The Lavo Kingdom was christened,
Before the experts arrived
In your community unearthing, enthralled
When you showed up
With a remnant of yourself;
A wrist – a crusty mottled grey relic
Which I had unwittingly
Muttered a greeting
Past the glass panel,
Past this inscrutable passage
Spanning three thousand years.
Your enduring bangle, a clue-giver –
Whispering a beam of knowledge
Weaving us back
To this shared narrative of
Our earthly sojourn.

Ellen Chia

The Spider in the Bathtub

They're drawn to bathtubs' sheer sides
in search of an anchor to spit their webs,
but realize, too late, their fatal error
and try to scramble out, into the safe,
right-angled world, but always fall back,
exhausting themselves.

Smooth's no joy to spiders; they find
no purchase in smooth, as we do:
in bedsheets, my Jerry Garcia tie,
the way a G & T slides down,
or a silky sax solo.

This spider is maybe despairing,
maybe regathering strength
for yet another attempt to scale
what amounts to an ice cliff
without the requisite climber's axe.

Me? I'd take the easy way out,
and smack it, toss it in the trash,
but Beth's made of kinder stuff,
and retrieves the lidded jar she keeps
to trap and free them into our backyard,
so they can hunt again.

Beth smiles, having saved one small,
useful life, but now she's on the ruthless
lookout for the ants that invaded in June,
the line needing to be drawn somewhere.

Robert Cooperman

The Old Man Warns the Young Man at the Bar

Flatback Sally come a whole new woman
Once that sun go down. Run over this little town
Just like a glance. Careful, young man, she might
Just fall on you. Be careful how you do –
That girl's all mouth and swallows and swears
Hell burns the bottom of her throat. Bears
Silence well, but that don't mean she hears.
Listen, Flatback Sally got nothing no man needs.
Let a good girl be your vessel: Sally bleeds
For men to stop her spilling. You should know
When girls like Sally bleed, it's all for show.
What smile she shows, there's twice that grimace hid,
Her porchlight eyes like lures. Believe me, kid –
Sally may look purty there, beneath you, on her back.
Like moonlight on steel teeth. A new-laid trap.

Rachel Custer

My Doctor & Dostoyevsky

My physician had just finished his pepperoni
pizza when I entered his cubby hole of an exam
room to give blood, a can of Diet Dr. Pepper

on his desk. I sat down in a comfy art deco chair
and we said our basic greetings before he began
chatting on Agatha Christie, which mystery

I can't remember, but she's old territory for us.
It never takes long for Fyodor to appear either,
a comforting Karamazov or, this time, by way

of a BBC film, Raskalnikov. "We don't know
what we want," one of us said, behind closed
doors, of course. My doctor also has good taste

in art: rather than paintings hanging of artificial
gazebos, Rembrandt and Whistlers gaze down
from the old plastered walls. "All your patients

must appreciate your moody art during exams,"
I said. Doc chuckled: there were no phony
flowers in a waterless vase, no *Living* magazine

spread out like a fan across a wicker table.
Eventually we both sighed about our plights,
upcoming elections, the loss of civility roaming

our big city streets, and I laid down gingerly on
the exam table, rolling up my shirt sleeve. Doc
(and I know I'll never have a better one no matter

how old I live) quipped and turned to ready his
needle, necessary unfortunately – he wasn't one
to do unnecessary tests or treatments. "Well, Tim,

let's see what's riding around in your red rivers,"
he said, hovering over me and starting to feel for
a vein with some difficulty, since mine don't show

easily. I was already queasy. "Just talk more about
Dostoyevsky," I told him. "That'll keep my mind
in a safe place, away from the drawing of blood. So

he does: "That scene where he drops the axe down
on her skull, in the BBC version I mean, nothing
at all sloppy about it." I could see the thin butterfly

needle sticking down into the joint of my arm, feel
it sucking a slow liquid from me. "Now hang in
there, Tim." Doc let his lips go. "Growing up in Kiev

I learned even elections can be quite bloody. You've
got to stand firmly, or lie down in your case. Don't
let a little bloodletting get to you. Don't let them see

you sweat. Or faint. And next time package that thing
up. Hepatitis B isn't fun. Neither gonorrhea or the clap.
If you've got to have one, Chlamydia trachomatis

would be the way to go. I'm going to go ahead and get
a second vial to test for syphilis – a lot of poets get
that one, you know. We read all this Fyodor and then

commit a grand Dmitry anyway, don't we? Okay, let's
bandage this up and then get some urine. I'm going
to bank on you being free of all these ugly squires."

37

As I said, Doc was my favorite. Not just the best doctor,
but probably the best person to talk to period. If only
he'd seen I was momentarily spared all talk of literature

and politics, for under the free arm stretched across
my pallid face I had conked out, couldn't hear a thing.

Timothy B. Dodd

Prayer for Walter

found walking
with very straight
legs but no angels
to flay the night
soft as he vaults
over gutters
once strutted
with exquisite
tigers to shrivel
and flame down
the arc of his
hand as he feels
for the wall and
the grains of
grace dropped:
I would lavish a
wasting condition
upon thee, slather
your hair with safety
and retreat and have
thee to lie down,
and stay down,
and sleep.

Matt Dennison

A Part of the Main

My enlarged prostate is strangling
my urethra the way Boris Karloff
strangles Ernest Thesiger in *The Ghoul*.

In the middle of the night, I can't
even make it to the toilet.
I fill empty mason jars that

I leave on the bedside table.
One day I trapped an ordinary
house spider in one of the jars,

filled it with pee during the night,
awoke at dawn to find the spider
floating in amber like that astronaut

in *2001* who got locked out
of the capsule and drifted,
arms and legs akimbo, into space.

On the island of Kauai I was
confronted by a huge cane spider
on the stucco wall of a rented condo.

I couldn't bring myself to kill it
because the intricate design on its back
resembled the swirling island designs

tattooed around the muscular arms
of Poipu surfers. The spider
seemed to belong there more than I.

Once on an island off the coast
of Belize, I came back from the beach
to find a black jungle spider

the size of my palm on the door
to the bathroom. I really had to pee.
So I smacked it to the ground

with my snorkel mask and crushed it
with my rubber fins. The Rorschach's
design its guts made on the floor tiles

looked like gun moll Gloria Grahame's
face after Lee Marvin threw
a pot of hot coffee at her

in *The Big Heat*, the same movie
in which Glenn Ford's wife and daughter
get blown up in a car bomb

meant for him because Ford was getting
too close to cracking an extortion racket.
Where did Glenn Ford belong?

He quit the force in anger, so
he wasn't a cop anymore, yet
he still staked out the gangsters

like a trapdoor spider who waits
for the right moment to spring
from the ground and devour his prey,

which reminds anyone who's seen it
of that demented preacher Robert Mitchum
played in *Night of the Hunter*, where he

41

stalks the children of his nemesis,
love and hate tattooed on alternate knuckles,
serenading them with a creepy hymn

that no one can sing to God anymore
without thinking of Mitchum's satanic
hyper-calm glare. Mitchum did it

because he didn't belong anywhere
but prison and, like Charlie Manson,
he would do anything to get back in.

It's not pee but a glass of plain water
that the child in *Signs* leaves around
the house and that turned out to be

the only way to kill the spider-like
aliens that invaded her father's cornfields.
It's hard to watch that movie now

because it stars that alleged anti-Semite
Mel Gibson who doesn't really belong
among the liberal Hollywood elites

such as Tom Hanks, who played a FedEx
executive that gets stranded on an
uncharted island in the middle of the Pacific.

Tom Hanks certainly doesn't belong
on that island, but just where
does he belong? – in *Catch Me If You Can*,

perhaps, where he plays the clever G-man
who pursues the spidery Leo DiCaprio.
Hanks, a diabetic, probably has an enlarged

prostate, too, which is strangling
his urethra in the worst way.
Sometime soon he may find himself

awake in the middle of the night
wishing he had a jar to pee in
because he's not going to make it

to the toilet, which is where pee belongs.
All of this to say that (much as I hate
to admit it) John Donne was probably

right when he said no man is an island
because each of us belong to one
another whether we like it or not,

including spiders and enlarged glands
and demented preachers and the numerous
islands that presume to separate us.

David Denny

salamander flux

he who was wearing the two lobsters was
a drunk sexy big-dicked young man, and except
for the two lobsters and the string
that connected them, he was totally naked.
**

this was supposed to have a been a lobster dinner
for two.
at his place.
just him and his new boyfriend.
but,
his boyfriend had cancelled on him,
with only mysterious reasons for the
cancellation. vague and mysterious reasons.
**

so,
now,
the drunk sexy big-dicked young man was wearing
two lobsters and the strings
that held them in place, and nothing else.
after he'd got the news of the cancellation,
he'd thought it would be fun to tie the two lobsters around his
waist.
hang one in front of his genitals, and hang the other
down the crack of his butt.
so he got some string, and, tying it to the claws,
he hung one lobster down across his genitals, and the
other lobster down across his buttcrack.
the heads of the lobsters were pointing up.
their tails were pointing down.
these lobsters had been cooked.
these lobsters were bright red.
these lobsters had cooled down enough
not to burn him, but they were still a bit warm.
**

so now he walked around in his apartment, all alone.
it was such a pretty evening,

the stars so bright,
the moon so splendid,
the feel of lobster shell
against
his own sweaty manflesh
so
well,
goddamn awful, in
the sexy way that sex can
be wonderfully awful, like love,
and hunger, and comfort, all
the things that he wanted,
but here he was, alone, with
just these two lobsters, and a bit
of string, and
the goofy look on his
face was almost
terror.

Carl Miller Daniels

j. bell's balls

smug people know everything, but they're not telling.
they purse their lips tellingly, but they don't tell.
they just know. have everything figured out.
all of it. everything makes sense to them.
**

smug people make the sexy big-dicked teenage boy
kind of nauseous.
they create a metallic taste on the tip of his tongue.
when the sexy big-dicked teenage boy is jerking off,
he tries not to think about them, but sometimes
he does anyway. when the sexy big-dicked teenage boy
thinks about them while jerking off, his
orgasms are never as good as they are
when he thinks about other things.
**

his favorite thing to think about
while jerking off is jamie bell.
jamie bell is the actor who starred
in *billy elliot* and *the chumscrubber*
and *mr foe* and *the eagle* and
other good movies, too.
jamie bell is 26. jamie bell
is hot sexy smoldering gentle
sweet with kind eyes and great lips
and perfect nipples.
the sexy big-dicked teenage boy
thinks about jamie bell a lot,
and, when the sexy big-dicked teenage boy
is jerking off, he imagines that
jamie bell is doing the same thing,
and that they are watching each other do it,
saying sweet gentle encouraging
intimate things to each other while
they are watching each other jerk off.
**

they are standing so close to each

46

other they can smell each other's breath.
they have both been eating peppermint candy,
and drinking vodka.
**

the torrent of hot sweet
high-voltage orgasm is going to shake
both
the sexy big-dicked teenage boy
and jamie bell
to the very fiber of their sweet gentle
sexual selves.
**

whenever the sexy big-dicked teenage boy
jerks off while thinking about jamie bell,
he knows what's going to happen next.
**

GOD! GOD! GOD! oh good gushy GOD!
**

he knew it would be good, and it was.
**

he's never smug about it, though.
**

god how he hates smug people.
**

they just make him sick.

Carl Miller Daniels

Picker

that's what they called him
a finger buried deep in his nose
as a way to cope
with a flabby stomach
& a face covered with so much acne
that it was about as baby soft
as the surface of mars

that was before everyone had anxiety
when ptsd was reserved for people with real problems
when kids threw lit matches at anyone
they couldn't just burn at the stake
when we ate pop rocks & pepsi
because we wanted to spontaneously combust
as if daring god to give it his best shot

his sister sat in the back of the bus
hiding from her own bloodline
denying his existence
to sit next to cheerleaders
who would shoot spitballs
into her greasy black hair
when she wasn't looking

she would just laugh
as if she was in on the joke
saving her tears for after supper
when she could write it all down
in a secondhand trapper keeper
with a wrinkled picture
of mary lou retton
taped to the front

they used to jump rope
in their front yard
with these same kids

their mother used to tell them
they could be whatever they wanted

but she never had to carry
their books in the snow
heavy with the weight of hours

when silence greeted them
in crowded halls

& blood seemed thicker
than almost anything.

John Dorsey

Poem for Curtis Hayes

you say that everything we can see here
was once a strawberry field
& talk about a girl
who once had a baby in the bathroom
that now has a busted sink
as we sit beside your empty swimming pool
sipping gin & tonics in the sun

the past is a young man's game
its bones good & strong

runaway birds in our infancy
we all make strange sounds
that pass for stories

before we fly away.

John Dorsey

Proverbs

three chinese boys
under a tarp in a pickup truck
in the desert
aren't bad hombres

they're just boys

you can't throw
fortune cookie wisdom
at the dead

a quiet rain
will say anything it pleases
to a hawk
on its deathbed

the song inside a pebble
was once a rock.

John Dorsey

My Prayer

Please, dear God, hear my plea,
do this little thing for me:

take a dump
on Donald Trump.

It's really not so much to ask,
I'm confident you're up to the task.

After all, you're not some helpless clod;
you're God,

and he's so full of shit
I'd like to see him wearing it.

W.D. Ehrhart

Saturday Matinee

I'm eleven years old alone
at the Alvin Theater,
a noisy kid-filled place
AKA "the monkey house,"
when I bump into a girl I know
from my aunt's neighborhood.
We're watching Roy Rogers
and Dale Evans on screen.
Diane is not interested in the movie
because she wants to talk about boys.
She's explaining her knowledge
of the birds and the bees to me,
and uses gross words
I've never heard before,
and she sees I'm not catching on,
so she goes into more yucky detail.
I want to tell her S*top,
I don't want to hear anymore*,
but I'm too shy.
I never see her again,
but a lifetime later,
I can still hear her
whisper in the darkness.

Barbara Eknoian

Elena Says

Elena has news. Elena has amazing,
great, big news.

Not all of life is tragedy.   I want
you to know me,

Elena says.   My drunk heart
in the old countries.

I want your hot barehanded grip
on my neck, your mouth

to my ear, and the words of the book
we cannot write.

Elena says she is a good girl.
A church girl.

A save-the-world girl.   The men
say *Elena, Elena*

Elena, you are still beautiful. The nets
of their hands

waiting to catch her spectacular,
fevered, fainting.

It is not her fault Elena can't take that body off.

I am trying to help us be friends,
she says, but how

can you just gaze above fire
like there is no fire?

Your silence is the lull between bell
tolls, asleep

in its own tepid water.
You've never even heard

me sing!   This sun in my throat
and how it rises,

and all the dark things that exit.
Tell me now,

your favorite song.   Show me
your monster, the interior

you.   Can't you see?
The tips of the waves are frothing,

and you are
always a deep sea

away. I just keep having big news
to share. Just now

a bird has landed on the bare wrist
of a branch. It is so wonderful, Elena

says, how it springs so gently inside
of its own weight.

It is all I can do to make you see it.

Kate Hanson Foster

"This light moist cake is just heavenly," shares
Milagro DeMilagros of Los Angeles, CA

Heavenly Angel Food Cake

First, separate the egg yolks.
Set aside or send them off
like a dozen monks.

Let the whites sit like Quakers
at room temperature for 30 min.,
as humble as a bowl of spit.
Let them reflect upon themselves.

Meanwhile, sift the sugar
and flour together 3 times.
Infuse the earth with lofty thoughts:
1 part substance, 3 parts air.

Now, return to the whites,
which should be foaming
or speaking in tongues.
Beat them hard like a Puritan.

Whip them into something more
than this, their basest form, and
watch the transformation –
from frothy dribble to cherub's robe.

First soft crescents swell in
gentle willingness, like virgins
bow their heads in reverence.

With each turn their zeal multiplies.
Slowly, gloved hands emerge and push
upward toward the skies.

Just as they aspire to their stiffest peaks,
anoint them with oils of almond and vanilla
and let the essence permeate.

Now, adding a little at a time,
fold the flour gently into the whites.
Batter should be airy and delicate.

Lightly spoon into a pan.
Cut through the batter with a knife
to remove any pockets of sin.

Cake should rise.

Andrea Fry

Rosalind Goldsmith

Helvetica

A tough story. How to frame it? Readers wanted a personal gloss, a current of compassion but not a flood. A tricky balance to strike on a story like this – a homeless boy who'd been arrested for forcing people at knifepoint to take cash out of their ATMs. It would be his column for tomorrow. Wednesday now and he hadn't started yet – 1,500 words to get down before 3:00. Possible? Of course. Just had to sort out the events, shimmy the facts into place, frame the lead, quotes from witnesses, one woman grievously injured and still in intensive care.

It was 9:30. He sat at his desk with his espresso and switched on his laptop, swiveling in his chair and sipping from the paper cup. Too sweet – must cut back on sugar – still – not. Opened a document – Helvetica. What? How did that get there? Switched to Times New Roman. Began to type. Where he'd start?

With the boy, of course. And stay with him. Homeless, hopeless, addicted lost boy in treacherous, blind-eyed city full of people who couldn't see him – or refused to. Or – the boy – invisible? Yes. Backspace backspace. Sixteen, living on the streets for two years already, his short life all cased up and locked away in the past, no future. So why did he? Why not? How could he not, considering – yes. Go with this.

Sympathy all with the boy. Not that he didn't care about the victim – but he wanted to be honest about this – his mantra for whatever he wrote: careful observation and absolute, marrow-deep personal honesty. So, to be honest here, he felt sorrow for the boy, though of course he could not excuse his crimes – the woman – six stab wounds to her torso – might not survive.

His fingers clicked away on the keyboard and the story began to take shape. He was tired from a late night out last night, didn't get home until 2:00, his wife on the couch, waiting and aggrieved. But – as he told her – these late nights were vital for him – gave him a chance to blow off steam, and to learn what his friends and colleagues were thinking – crucial for his job – where they were trending, what threads he should pick up, which ones let drop. Irrelevancy happened so fast these days, you couldn't see it snatching your story away. You had to keep up – even on the local stories – so –

She understood. After a long talk – the same long talk every time – she always got it in the end. So: Sleep: 3:30.

58

Now, here. Staring at the screen through a patina of exhaustion and caffeine. Loved his job, though, loved it, loved the people here. How rare. How lucky he was. He knew it, told himself so, almost every day. This was – *it* – what life was about, wasn't it? A job you love, co-workers you respect and care for, a family – well, kids not yet, but soon soon – and enough of an income to be comfortable. What luck. Really. What joy.

And more: his take on the articles he wrote – always the human – lift – that raised the story above the facts. The human blood, the human blunders, the living breathing heart, the blood life that lay behind the catastrophe of each story – this he never failed to get at. Even in the worst of them, the very worst of humanity. He felt for them and was known for it. A lot of nasty messages came his way on Facebook and Twitter, accusing him of implausible, misplaced – even false – sympathy, of forging his career on that sympathy, of condoning and even revering monsters. But he knew monsters didn't exist. They were all human. There was always something behind, above, underneath – all around them: the structure of violence as invisible as air. He wrote hundreds of pages on this: on how the unseen cradle of violence rocked children into young criminals, how they became lost, irretrievable adults. He sold papers on this, yes, but more – he wanted others to see things the way he saw them. Really. If at all possible.

Compassion. We must have compassion for the worst of humanity. If not, we cannot forgive ourselves. Forgiveness was the key.

He structured the story around the facts of the boy's tragic childhood – his years growing up in the impoverished barren suburbs, an abusive addicted father, a mother who worked two jobs just to survive. Never breakfast, rarely lunch. At school, hungry and ignored – above all – this: the horrific neglect on all sides: mother, father, teachers, the city council, the state: no one saw this boy, no one paid any attention to him, as if he was already lost before ten, dead before fourteen, when – the appeal of a local gang overwhelming him – he took to injecting, to stealing for them and for the validation they readily gave him, a validation he'd never had before from anyone. He could use a few quotes here, from a former school mate who remembered him as "shy, quiet, but never violent." Maybe he was bullied? Probably so.

The background story was like a thousand other background stories, a hundred thousand. These abandoned kids – a battalion – no – a city – no – an entire population of wasted life, wasted potential, lost souls all of them. How could you not have compassion for him, for all of them – no matter what their crimes? They'd grown up with violence all around them. It was in their mother's milk, their father's blood. In the air they breathed. In the cheap walls of their poorly built apartment blocks. As we do not live within this structure of violence, we are able to see it, and we must absolve, we must find remedy.

Now the result of this crime: the woman. The exact state of her being now: on an IV, blood transfusions, two operations already, a lacerated liver, intestines, the lower colon removed. Fifteen stitches in her face and on oxygen. Will she survive? Her brother saying: "She's the most generous, kind person I know. She didn't do anything wrong, never hurt anyone. We're devastated." Her innocence though – even her tragic wounds – still no justification for the neglect and abuse this boy has suffered. He is society's child. Society's neglect has created this little "monster." And is responsible for this crime. He'd get a torrent of tweets on that sentence, he knew it, but what the – . Society must take responsibility, fix the problem. And society must first forgive. For without forgiveness, we cannot move forward, we cannot even hope to survive. Hmm.

The journalist sat back, thinking: Forgive. Ok. He'd written the book on this, right? Literally. This should be easy – two paragraphs on this – and –

The book he'd written, *Letting It Go: A Radical Approach to Forgiveness*, came out of a blog he'd started years ago, which was just about his day-to-day problems and frustrations and how he'd had trouble with his family growing up. Not that he'd been poor – the opposite – but his father, a prominent corporate CEO, was mostly absent, his two older brothers tormented him mercilessly and "sabotaged" his childhood, as he put it. His mother, a depressive inept caregiver who needed more care than she could give – a weeper – incapable of solving anything and exhausted – she left the kids to themselves. And he always got the brunt of it. And there was no one to stop the "abuse," as he named it.

Interesting – the blog started off as a rant, blaming everyone, full of rage and vitriol and accusation. His brothers stopped speaking to him after one particular post which detailed an outing in the car from their cabin in the Laurentians to a local lake for a picnic. His brothers – both of them – nearly drowned him. And although he wasn't sure if it was intentional, he lived in terror of them ever since.

He got one email from his eldest brother after this entry. "This never happened." was all it said. Never heard from him again. The other brother, who had once punched him in the stomach, had stopped all communications years ago. Not even any Christmas cards or birthday cards from either of them. Just that one cold, lying email.

It was after that email that the journalist began to read books on Zen, self-improvement, living in the present moment, forgiving and so on. The tone of his blog began to change until he forgave his mother, his father, his two brothers and everyone else in the world. He began to write – instead of hate, frustration and blame – how forgiveness had come into his life and ignited his heart, like an epiphany, and how it changed everything.

Out of this, on the advice of a friend, he wrote the small volume *Letting It Go: A Radical Approach to Forgiveness*. Reviews by authors of similar books were glowing, and to his surprise, the book became a national best seller. And since then, things got easier in his life. He got this job at the *Post*. And forgiveness – this thing that had become him and that he had become – entered into every one of his articles one way or another. Somehow, though he never said this to anyone, the warmth of this idea – this feeling – helped him in every single aspect of his life, especially his marriage – since he was continually forgiving his wife. He even forgave his two brothers for their silence, their absence, their refusal and their betrayal.

From an angry, resentful and bitter teenager he became a responsible, loving happy adult. He was – someone else now. At times he barely recognized his own joy, his own good will towards others, his contentment. He never could have dreamed he would become this person.

Yet here he was – story nearly done now, espresso drained. Lunch soon. At the café down the street. He was beginning to feel hungry. He'd go now, come back, edit the shit out of this story and have done with it.

He chucked his coffee cup in the bin, shut down his laptop, grabbed his phone and ran down the three flights of stairs to the lobby – had to get more exercise – true – maybe a gym membership? Or some kind of a running club? Hmm. Maybe he could fit that in on a Friday evening, or –

He stepped out the front door of the building into brilliant sunshine. Lunch. No. first – a – on his way to the café, he stopped off at a convenience store for a lottery ticket for his wife. She bought these things all the time, though he never did – didn't believe in luck at all – but she always liked getting an extra one from him. And especially since their tiff last night, so – yes.

He opened the glass door to the convenience store and stood behind a kid at the counter. Young kid, he noticed, younger than fifteen. He always noticed details. Once thought he'd be a good spy – if his career as a journalist tanked, if he became redundant, he'd apply for a job at CSIS or even the CIA – how does one go about doing that, actually –

that's an interesting question – you couldn't just apply – or maybe you could, but –

He saw the kid grab a Mars bar and slip it into his pocket while the cashier was scanning his purchase of a Coke. "Hey," the journalist said.

The kid froze. Then leaned forward on the counter his back tense and hunched. The cashier gave him his change and he pocketed it.

"You should put that back."

The boy turned to him. An insolent combative face. A face that was just waiting to convulse into a yell. The kid just stood there, inches away from the journalist.

"Put what back?" the cashier said.

"A Mars bar. I just saw him take it."

"Bull shit, creep," said the boy.

The journalist just stood there, calm. "Look," he said, "Just put it back, and I think no one will pursue this, right?" He nodded to the cashier and the cashier nodded back. "Ok, it's all good," he said, extending his open hands in front of him, towards the boy. "Just – "

The boy stabbed his finger into the journalist's chest. "You're a bullshit little bitch. You fucking can't accuse me of anything. I never took a fucking thing, right – asshole?" He didn't take his finger away. Pressed it in harder.

This kid talked like a thug, couldn't be more than fourteen years old. Sixteen at the outside. It was laughable. "Take your hand off me," he said.

"Why should I?" said the boy.

The journalist saw the boy's nose that looked broken or flattened, like dripping wax. His eyes flashing scorn, defiance.

"Who do you think you fucking are, dude? An Asshole, right? Asshole?"

It was pathetic how the boy was trying to be a grown-up thug. Pathetic. He could laugh it was so pathetic. He could laugh. Because. Really. It was laughable.

The light got white hot bright in that store. Could be the sun, or an electrical surge. He noticed the change in the light, the heat, just before he grabbed the boy by his collar and lifted him off his feet. He slapped him hard across the face, right – left, dropped him, punched him in the stomach. The boy collapsed onto the floor. He started to kick him in the stomach, and when the boy folded up like crumpled paper, he kicked him in the head. "No!" he heard from very far away.

He picked the boy up off the floor and smashed him up against the glass door, pushed him into it again and again, pulling him back then slamming him into the heavy glass, the boy's head hitting the glass hard. It cracked. Blood started to flow from the boy's head and ran down the glass, pooling on the floor. Blood was draining from the boy's nose, the mouth opened. A vomit of blood came out of that mouth and spattered over his shirt. He could feel the wetness of it. He looked at the boy's eyes. They were glazed, unseeing eyes. Those eyes could not see him now. Painted china eyes.

He let go and the boy dropped to the floor in a small heap. He opened the door and stepped out onto the street. His hand was bloody. His shirt covered in blood.

He stared at his hand a moment and looked up. The street was empty. The sun hot. The thing was to – he was on the way to – the story. Yes. Finish the story. But a question he had to answer first. What was it? What was this question? Something about Helvetica? Was it that? No. A question about the story. It was – a vital question. He had to answer it. Right now.

A Landscape in Poland

You can still walk out there
And stand among the white trunks of the birch trees.
No snow yet on the ground, and the railroad tracks
Leading into that forest are old, covered with rust.

The trees are dense, and blend together
Like smoke from a great fire that has smoldered
Underground for a long time. No one will notice you
Lurking near what appears to be an abandoned factory

On the other side of the woods. Will there be
Derelict boxcars overgrown with weeds,
Their doors thrown open? Huge chimneys
Are probing around in the sky

For a light as cold and pale as the face of a child.
Silence, and yet there are voices here too,
As if the birch trees were speaking quietly
In a language known only to themselves.

There is one window high up in a wall
Of the abandoned factory. At times
You will see shadows flit behind the pane.
And then someone will come to the window and gaze out.

Jay Griswold

Ode to Vladimir Mayakovsky

Vladimir Mayakovsky was a real live wire.
His verses after 2 AM
Glowed like candles in a cathedral,
And when he shouted obscenities
It could light up the Brooklyn Bridge.

Vladimir Mayokovsky was ten feet tall
And had a heart as big as a house.
Sometimes he would set the house on fire
And then leap out of himself.

Snowflakes are falling.
Wolves are loping over the Steppes.
Wolf, what happened at Tanguska
Vladimir! Vladimir Mayokovsky!

Vladimir Mayakovsky was a prodigious lover,
But the woman he loved most of all was Russia.
How brightly he burned when he mounted a cloud
And just flew around in the darkness ...

Jay Griswold

Dinner and Peaches with Grandma Pressey – the 1950s

I remember
back in the 'fifties
my grandma would say
all that's on the plate
is all there is.
Don't waste nothing.

She'd say
if you're still hungry
sneak off
to Mr. Johnson's place.
Half a block up Melrose.

His peach tree's
coming in.
Hanging over the sidewalk
don't break no branches
don't take none to waste.
Other folks might need
a bite too.

If he comes out
yelling
tell him Mrs. Pressey
says
thank you
and run like hell.

Bill Gainer

What Anyone Knows

Robert's twin sister calls
to tell me that their mom died.
I offer condolences, ask
when did it happen. Twenty
years ago, I'd see her
as she regularly visited
Robert at the group home
and I learned where Robert
got his sweetness, his warmth.
Recently, we'd drive him out
to Long Island for extended
weekend stays five, six times
a year. I'd sit at my desk, watch
his eyes light up as he blew sloppy
kisses and mumbled he loved her too
on his weekly phone call. Joanne
wants to know what we should do
about Robert, the guy who was pulled
out of the womb after her. Diagnosed
with mental retardation and cerebral
palsy, he spent his early childhood
in Willowbrook hell. She wonders
how much of it he'd understand,
what would happen when he saw
his mom lying in the coffin, whether
he'd kick and yell, throw himself
on the floor when it was time
to leave, would he ever stop
crying. I wonder what anyone
knows about death, but tell her
I think he should participate.
No one knows how much
Robert understands anything
since he can't tell you himself,
but I feel sure that sitting
in the church with the organ

mourning, the incense rising
as they close the casket
will be something he'll remember
whenever he goes home
to his family and never sees
his mom again no matter
how many times he asks
and he'll make some kind
of connection. I tell her
we'll put on his suit, sit
nearby and help him
with anything he needs,
and he'll get through
that day the same way
he gets through his life.

Tony Gloeggler

What Work Really Is

Friends ask why stay? You turn
sixty-five in June, live in a rent
controlled apartment, can afford
to retire. It's an hour and a half
bus and subway commute each
way between Queens and Red Hook.
The new executive director looks
like Michelle Obama, acts like
Donald Trump. Long time
workers have been forced
to leave, support staff laid off,
care compromised. You'll miss,
no mourn, this place, the people
who work, who live here, taken
from Willowbrook as teens,
integrated into the community.
Your friends say their lives
have been better because
you wound up here. You know
all they've meant to your life.
Though you never believed
anything was meant to be,
you recognize how unlikely
it was you found your way
here, stayed forty years, helped
shape this home into something
you consider sacred? You tell
friends, you don't want to stay
home, write. You've always
found time for that and nobody
is dying, waiting for anyone's poetry.
You're worried, afraid loneliness
could deepen, boredom escalate.

Tamara yells from down the hall.
She needs help getting Larry
to the bathroom. *One, two, three.*
Up. Take a breath. *Steady?* Now,
help him shuffle to the toilet.
You latch his hands around
the towel rack, grab hold
under his arms. She bends,
pulls, and yanks his pants
all the way down when Larry
clearly says "*I got it.*" Tamara,
you, look at each other. His first
words since advanced dementia.
You both crack up, land high fives
as she tears his under-alls off, starts
to wash his pale, shrunken ass.

Tony Gloeggler

Bed Time

She can't sleep, keeps
getting up to check
window locks, door
knobs, sits in the kitchen,
smokes cigarettes. Back
in bed, she wraps both
arms around her knees,
clenches them tight
to her chest. He reaches
for the light. She turns
away and he starts
to stroke her hair.
She tells him to stop,
please. He's sorry, asks
can he hold her.
She breathes deep, feels
his arms around her

And she tastes the leather-gloved hand
strapped across her mouth again. Her face
slams against the garage wall and that voice
hisses *don't make a sound* as he tugs and tears
at her clothes. He shoves a knee between her legs,
spreads her thighs wider with a fist. His cock
rips her open, pumps harder and faster, spits
inside her with a shudder. He steps back, starts
to run and her mouth yells and yells and yells

For help. He brings
her closer, holds her
softly, whispers
it's alright sweetheart,
sshh, try to sleep.
He rocks her slowly.
She tries to shut
her eyes, feels
his cock pressed
against her ass.

Tony Gloeggler

Alexis Garcia

Specks of Dust

"We're here," Tony said.

I looked out the window and stared at the only two-bedroom house in the neighborhood with peeling brown paint, and a lawn full of yellow, prickly things that used to be called grass.

"You sure you don't want to get breakfast?" I said as my left hand hovered over my mouth. Tony won't let me leave a toothbrush. He won't let me leave anything at his place. One time I tried to leave my baby blue cardigan underneath his bed. But his stupid cat, Melvin, started playing with it and left it exposed on the floor. Tony noticed my cardigan right away, grabbed it, and called out, "Hey!" from his doorway. He jogged down the hall to hand it over. And the motherfucker had the decency to smile at me as if he was doing *me* a favor. I rolled my eyes and stomped away in disappointment. He didn't call out to find out what was wrong.

"Huh?" He said, looking down, scrolling through his phone.

"Do you want to get breakfast?" I said.

"You're mumbling," he said. He didn't even look up at me. He just kept scrolling. I looked at the house again; the black tape over the hose was coming undone.

"I'm hungry," I said louder. My hand still hovered.

"Oh, Laura," he said. Tony rolled his eyes away from his phone screen onto me. He finally looked at me, but I still felt unacknowledged.

"I can't. I have work," he said.

I sank into my seat. I wanted to believe if I sank as much as possible, I would shrink. Only then could I leave this car, this situation, this mental state. I would swim forever inside the forgotten potholes in front of the driveway.

"It's the weekend though," I said.

"There are no weekends when you are a 9th grade Social Science teacher. I have to finish grading the scantrons, worksheets, the quizzes. Not to mention the lesson plan for Mon—," he said.

"I get it," I cut him off. I felt lightheaded. My stomach was queasy. I couldn't tell if I was more repulsed with him, or myself.

"I just have a professional career, baby," he said. Tony put his hand over my thigh.

"I'll call you later," he said. He squeezed my thigh, hard.

73

I thought of all the things I wanted to say to him. Instead, they all crashed into each other like cars at an intersection. So I decided to say something fast than nothing at all.

"You went to the local state university for Christ sakes," I said.

"What kind of professional adult hangs out at the same shitty dive bar for the past year on the weekends anyways," I said.

I opened the passenger door of his '08 white Toyota Camry. I stuck my left leg out and pulled myself up out of the car. I immediately was yanked back into my seat. I tried lifting myself again, but I only fell back. I kept tugging and something kept pulling. I grinded my teeth and felt the blood rush to my cheeks. Perhaps it was the buried resentment. Or the shameful yearning of wanting Tony. I looked down. It was neither. My belt was still buckled.

I unbuckled myself and slammed the door. I didn't feel satisfied, so I reopened the door and slammed it as hard as I could. I heard Tony yell, *Jesus!* Fuck him.

"Laura!" Tony yelled out the window.

Unfuck him.

I turned around. Even though my candy red, Target brand high heels were killing my ankles, I tried my best to look composed. I was even hopeful enough to consider I looked sexy, despite wearing last night's clothing.

"You forgot your thong," he said. He held it up over the passenger seat with his index finger.

"Seriously?" I said. I snatched it from his finger and shoved it into my purse. I should have just turned around and walked away. But it was the only underwear I own that doesn't have a hole.

I opened the front door and Jeremy is asleep on the couch. Even though the house had two bedrooms, we slept in the same bed. It started off with one of us having a nightmare. Then, the other one was dumped. Then, the other one was fired. Then, the other one said good-bye to their grandmother. Then, the other one's parent was diagnosed with liver cancer. Until sleeping next to each other became the only time we ever felt safe. However, for the past two weeks, Jeremy had been sleeping on the couch. It made our bed suddenly feel a lot wider, colder like I'm on the deck of a floating boat with no captain.

I plopped on the rocking chair and struggled to take off my high heels. I bought them a half a size smaller because they were on clearance. I grunted plenty of *Ow's* and *C'mon's* for Jeremy to shift his body. His back faced me. After I got the last high heel off, I slowly moved toward him to grab the remote under his armpit. I stepped over his cereal bowl that had leftover milk and a plastic, black spoon inside of it.

I grabbed the remote and went to sit back down. I pressed the power button on the remote, but the TV wasn't turning on. I opened the remote's battery compartment: empty. Jeremy inherited the house after his parents passed away. He asked me to move in with him because he thought it would convince him to keep the place together. We haven't been able to keep anything together.

"Hey, Jeremy," I whispered. No response

"Jeeeeer-meeee." I whispered a little louder. Still, no response.

"Goddammit, Jeremy. Wake up," I said. I wasn't whispering anymore. I tossed the empty remote at him. It hit his back. He moaned.

"You made it back," Jeremy said. His back was still facing me.

"Want to get something to eat? I'm bored," I said.

"What time is it?" he asked.

"I dunno. 930ish?" I said.

"Cool. McDonald's is still serving breakfast," he said.

"Number 38," the cashier said. Jeremy got up from our table and returned with a tray of wrapped food. He handed me two hash browns and a carton of orange juice.

I hunched over my food. My sunglasses were still on. I felt queasy again. Jeremy took a bite of his ham and cheese McMuffin.

"You're not hungry, babe?" he said with a mouth full of food. I shook my head.

"It was that bad huh?" he said.

I shrugged. I watched my breakfast get cold.

"I don't know why you still see him. You always say the sex is alright. He doesn't even want to date you," he said.

"So? You don't date half the dicks you suck," I said. I took my sunglasses off. The ambient lighting was more uncomfortable than usual.

"But I'm not trying to date them," he said. He shifted his head side to side in order to emphasis his point.

I flipped him off. He blew me a kiss.

"Babe. So can I have one then? Since you're not hungry and all," he asked as he looked down at my untouched hash browns.

I slid the tray to his side of the table.

"I still can't believe we ran into the woman Tony is actually getting married to. And I jus' cannot fuckin' get over that he never even mentioned it to you," he said.

I didn't say anything. I crossed my arms on the table and rested my head on top.

"Angela from high school. Who would have thought?" he said. He shrugged in disbelief. Then inhaled the hash brown.

"I mean," he said as he chewed. "The whole ... interaction was so ... so innocent," he said.

I let out a loud sigh as a cue for him to move on. He didn't.

"She didn't even seem suspicious of you. The only thing she could recall about you is always being with me underneath the football bleachers. When we would smoke weed out of the apples we stole from the cafeteria," he said. He chuckled.

"But you totally booked it to the restroom when she mentioned getting married to a high school teacher named Tony," he said. Jeremy searched the tray, looked at his hands, then wiped them on his jeans.

"I know," I said. I slammed my hands on table. "I was there," I said annoyed. The tone in my voice caught myself and Jeremy off-guard. I quickly lifted my hands off the table.

"I ... I'm sorry," I said.

Jeremy grabbed one of my hands. He interlocked his fingers with mine. We held hands in the air for a moment.

I met Jeremy in the 9th grade. We sat in the back during chemistry. I was the first one he told about liking boys. He made me promise to not tell anyone. I told him I would promise if he promised not to tell anyone that my dad, my real dad, molested me when I was six. We held hands for the rest of the class period. In the12th grade, Jeremy came out to everyone. He felt liberated, for a little while. Meanwhile, I still kept my secret between us two. He came out to his parents, my foster parents, our classmates, our teachers. He suddenly became likeable, popular for the rest of the school year. On time, he even chanted to me under the bleachers: *I'm free! I'm free! I'm free!* I envied him for it. I never felt free before, during, or after we shared our secrets. To me, being free felt like being Santa Claus, the Easter Bunny, God. It just never felt possible.

"I'm going to end it this time," I said. I felt thirsty. The statement had run so dry; I heard the words crumbling to dust in my throat. But I couldn't stop the sentence from running out of my mouth. I had to say it. Over, and over, and over until something new happened. But nothing new ever happened.

"I actually think he is jealous of her getting a PhD," I said.

"What? What makes you think that?" Jeremy said.

"The sex is getting more aggressive. And he wants me to be silent or scream in agony. Almost like he's trying to stab me from the inside to get rid of her. Or me. Or both," I said.

Jeremy looked sympathetic. Then, he shook his head like he was erasing what he had pictured.

"I love you, babe" he said. I pointed at my chest, then held up two fingers.

I stabbed the orange juice with the straw. I took a few sips, decided I was done, and handed the half empty carton over to Jeremy. He drank it in three gulps then tossed it onto the pile of scattered food paper and used napkins. We sat in silence. We watched the customers around us, eat, get up, throw away their food, leave. Then watched new customers repeating the same routine. The cashiers took the orders, asked the followed up questions, said thank you, and did it all over again. It felt like everyone had a cycle to follow, but we didn't. At least in that moment. We were lucky enough to be still for a minute. I wanted to take out my phone and ask someone to take our photo; so, we could always enjoy this minute. But the cycle didn't work that way. It never hesitated to take away from you again. Again. And again. In order to remind you, how insignificant you and everything around you is. Jeremy and I knew that. We always knew that. Yet, we continued to hold onto one another like our friendship was a peaceful protest against that. I felt my butt vibrate.

"Oh, crap. That's my alarm," I said. I took out my phone and turned the alarm off.

"I have to get ready for work," I said.

"Is Denise still having you clean toilets?" Jeremy asked as he put the trash on the trash.

"No. Thank God. I get to work concession today," I said. I grabbed the tray, dumped the trash into the trash bin, and set the tray on top of the bin.

"Bring home some popcorn again," Jeremy said. He held the door open for me.

I walked out and felt my chest get heavy. I thought about life's inevitable cycle, again.

I work at a movie theater sounded cool. Except, I was 28 years old and the only professional skills I had gained from the job was making popcorn, scooping popcorn, and sweeping popcorn. My manager, Denise, was a pompous 23 years old with two AA's and my co-workers were still in high school. Still, I tolerated them all pretty well. Until they started ranting about something I didn't care about or care to know about, which happened quite often. When it did, I always went out for a smoke break. I never actually considered smoking until a year ago. The act itself never seemed appealing. What seemed appealing was it was a *peaceful* act. Many people didn't approve of smoking anymore. So, I started to use it as an excuse to leave. To escape social situation and, be alone.

About two months ago, Denise offered me a job as a stand lead. Maybe if she hadn't scheduled me to clean the bathrooms for the past two weeks, I would have actually considered it. But I was mad. And the thought of having to work more with her made me madder. So I said, "This job is only temporary." I don't think she believed me. Especially since I'd been working for almost three years. She told me to think about it some more because this was a beneficial opportunity for my future. I didn't have to. There was no benefit. No future. So there was nothing to think about.

My favorite shifts were working the concession stand. I've always heard people say how much they like to walk along the beach shore. They would carry their shoes so the squishy, wet sand seeps between their toes. They explained it is romantic. Calming. Majestic, even. An exquisite moment of living. I never learned how to swim or enjoyed the sight of strangers' bare feet. So I couldn't understand what they meant until I started working behind the concession counter. I looked forward to taking customer's orders because it gave me a reason to walk over the spilled popcorn across the tiles. I imagined my feet would talk back to me every step I took like I was having an outer body conversation with myself. I'd hear the *crunch, crunch, crunch* below my shoe. It gave me validation. It was a sensation no other human could bring me, and no other human could take away from me.

Dylan and Rachel were working the stand with me. It was the usual busyness for a Saturday afternoon. When the lines finally died down, Dylan started refilling the popcorn machine and restocking the candy shelves. Rachel went on her fifteen minute break. I contemplated to help Dylan, but I didn't contemplate it too hard. I just stayed in front of the cash register: to appear ready for the next customers. I placed my elbows on the counter and rested my head in my palms. That's when I saw them.

They were holding hands, making eye contact, laughing. He never laughed with me. They were walking towards me. My teeth started grinding. I wanted them to stop, to turn around, and just fucking stop. But they didn't. I never saw him in a buttoned up, long sleeve with gel hair before. He wore his hair messy with and wrinkled t-shirts at the bar. However, my focus was more on Angela. My legs started shaking; my body temperature dropped. Her long, curled blond hair swayed side to side. She didn't have lipstick marks on her teeth. I imagined she had naturally symmetrical breasts. And her necklace was real silver, not the kind that rusts within two weeks. I'm sure she always remembered to brush her teeth in the mornings. Fuck them.

Rachel still wasn't back. And Dylan was occupied with restocking the nachos. Goddammit. Angela looked in my direction. I panicked and ducked behind the counter. I thought about crawling to the side and rush to the restroom. I took a deep breath and slowly crawled away from the cash register. I was halfway there until Dylan called out, "Aye dude! We got some customers!"

My heart sank into my stomach. I thought I was going to throw up. I started coughing uncontrollably instead. I got up fast and went to the soda dispensers to grab some water. I almost forgot about my situation until I turned around. They were standing right in front of the register.

"Hiiiiiiii. Welcoooome," I said with an open smile as I walked towards them. I wanted to stop smiling, but I couldn't. My smile only widened. I stretched out my arms as if I owned the counter, but it felt more like I was preparing to get crucified.

Tony's eyes bulged at me. He quickly looked down to his feet and rubbed the back of his neck.

"You know, I don't think I want any popcorn anymore," he said.

Angela ignored him. She gave me a look of concentration. She pointed at me with her mouth opened, but no words were spoken.

"That's it! You're Jeremy's friend!" She finally said. "I knew I recognized you."

I nodded too fast; it made me light headed. She sounded innocent. It made me wonder if I had any innocence left.

"Remember me? At The Cove? We talked for a bit?" she said with enthusiasm.

"Yeah ... I remember," I said, looking down at my hands. They looked pale and cold and almost frozen. I did not feel nervous anymore. I felt exhausted.

"Wait. How ... how do you guys know each other? What did you guys talk about?" Tony asked.

"We went to high school together," she said.

I nodded too slow this time. I looked at Tony. He squinted his eyes and pretended to read the menu.

"I didn't know you worked here. Are you the manager?" Angela asked. I chuckled.

"No, I've been working here for almost three years," I said.

"Ooh," she said. Her tone dropped. She wouldn't say it, but I could tell she was disappointed in me too.

"So what can I get you guys?" I said.

"Medium popcorn," Tony said fast. He still wouldn't make eye contact with me. His face and neck were red.

I nodded, turned around, grabbed one of the filled medium popcorn bags that laid under the light bulb.

"We want a fresh popcorn," Tony said. I paused with the popcorn in my hand. I wanted to throw the popcorn at his face. Instead, I said, "Right," out loud.

I looked over at them. Tony wrapped his arm around her and she kissed him on the cheek. My legs began trembling again.

I scooped popcorn from the machine and noticed none of the popcorn was going into the bag. I realized it was because each scoop had become more violent than the last. My scooping turned into jabbing. I didn't care. I jabbed harder into the mini mountain of popcorn until my entire body started thrusting back and forth with the jabs. I started sweating. I thought about slowing down or stopping, but my head felt disconnected from my body. Until finally, I was out of breath. I stared at the popcorn. My eyes watered and forehead was hot. I finished scooping the popcorn into the bag and turned around to them.

"That'll be eight dollars and eighty-nine cents," I said, quietly.

She handed me her card. That was when I got a glimpse her engagement ring. It had a huge diamond in the middle with smaller diamonds going around the band. I don't know anything about jewelry, but I could tell it was worth more than everything Jeremy and I own.

"I said I'd get it, hun," Tony said as he gently pushed her arm away from me.

He pulled out a twenty and placed it on the counter.

"Keep the change," he said. Tony finally made eye contact with me, but I stared down first. I looked at the twenty. My hands started to clinch into shaking fists. My mind was trying to swim back to my body, but it kept floating away. My body reclaimed itself and did whatever it thought was best.

"Lori, you have really great customer service. We don't mind," she said.

I slammed my hand on the counter over the bill.

"My name is not Lori. It's Laur-AH," I said. I chuckled between the words in my sentence. Or maybe it was my mouth trying to prevent myself from crying. I had been feeling insignificant for too long that I had to do something so fucked up to remind me I exist. First, it was selling my virginity for $300 over the internet. Then, it was wrecking my mom's boyfriend's truck. Then, it was fucking Tony. Then, it was falling for Tony. Then, it was fucking Tony after I found out he was married. Now, it was going to be confessing it to Angela. Right here. This was it.

I cleared my throat. "Oooh, by the way," I said with the fresh popcorn in one hand as I leaned the other on the counter. I didn't recognize myself; my voice sounded clear and confident.

"I just thought you should know …" I continued. I was ready. It was coming.

I looked at them; I shifted my eyes back and forth between them. They were each other's placebo effect of happiness. So, what was mine? It wasn't Tony. It wasn't the end of their relationship. Definitely not this job. And definitely, not this situation.

"I … I," I said. I took a deep breath, but it just made me feel more light-headed than before.

"I just thought you should know that … we're not allowed to take tips," I said. I took the twenty and placed it in the register.

"Here's your change," I said. I sat it on the counter instead of handing it to Tony. I didn't look up. I saw Tony's hand grab the change. They didn't say anything. They just walked away.

I collapsed my arms on the counter; my head followed.

Rachel finally came back and Dylan finished restocking. They started talking about Dylan's house party. The popcorn machine was cooking. So, they talked louder. I heard Rachel call out my name. I didn't respond. I lifted my head and saw a crowd of people walking towards us. I rolled my eyes away from them, got up from my position, and faced Rachel and Dylan.

"Are you going to Dylan's party this weekend? His parents will be out of town," Rachel said.

"Yeah, Laura! You should come. It's gonna be raging," Dylan said. He had a huge smile across his face as he nudged my side boob with his elbow.

"Maybe," I said, quietly.

Dylan and Rachel exchanged a look.

"Hey, so if we like all pitch in money," Rachel said.

"Would you buy us the alcohol?" Dylan said.

They didn't wait for me to answer. Instead, they talked about how drunk they were at the last party. The popcorn machine must have gotten louder because they started talking louder. The crowd of people began forming lines. They exchanged ideas with each other of what to order. I felt claustrophobic, but I still felt empty. Not even the dark, or the specks of dust inside of me could keep me company.

"I'm taking a smoke break," I said out loud as I rushed towards the back door to the alley behind the theater.

I stepped outside. I took deep breaths, hoping I could save as much air as possible for later. I leaned against the wall. My hands were trembling as I reached in my butt pocket and pulled out the carton and lighter. I tried focusing my hand to be still as it pulled out a cigarette. It was useless. I felt the tears flooding down my cheeks and meeting at the edge of my chin. My hair was in my face. I noticed my name tag was upside down. I was still wearing last night's makeup. I lit the cigarette, closed my eyes, and inhaled it. I was crashing, but I continued to stand.

Yearning

Her baby's hungry crying wakes her at three every morning. She carries him to the rocking chair to breastfeed him. When he falls back asleep in her arms, she contemplates his minute features under the bedside lamp: the baby's exquisite, soft lips resemble his father's, a nose looks like his brother's, and he has his sister's eyes and smooth hair. Looking at him, she sees not one person, but three.

At dawn, she lays him on the bed and gently wakes him. She traces her fingers over his lips, his nose, his eyes. She speaks to him as if she were waking his brother and sister for school, his father for work. Ever since they perished in a car accident three weeks ago, she's felt as if they have come back to life in his face.

Wafa Al-Harbi

translated from the Arabic by Essam M. Al-Jassim

Friday Night Boxing

Such poetic names for the fighters.

Kid Gavilan, his legendary "bolo punch,"
a compact version of the more ungainly "roundhouse right."

Jake LaMotta, Raging Bull,
street fighter who became middleweight champ.

And Rocky Marciano, the Brockton Blockbuster,
undefeated heavyweight champion of the world.
Could he ever be forgiven for humiliating
the aging Brown Bomber, Joe Louis?

Best of all was Sugar Ray Robinson
considered by many the greatest "pound for pound" fighter
there ever was and that includes Muhammad Ali.

Perhaps there was none sadder than Marcel Cerdan,
great French middleweight, killed in a plane crash
at the height of his career,
leaving behind a heartbroken Edith Piaf
who would never be the same.

Jersey Joe Walcott, Willie Pep and Sandy Saddler.
Chico Vejar …

All the violence, poetry, and drama
a ten inch screen could hold
in living rooms throughout America.

Alan Harawitz

And Yet the Strings

Again, a rainbow sprouting from your violin –
no, it's no light. You never wanted to mother.
Music was the way – adagios hanging from
the clouds. *But God had something in store –*

come on.

What happened was we were drinking herbal tea
and you told me of new pregnancy within these
silent walls of our favorite coffee shop and I said
I'm sorry, I'm sorry because I didn't know what

else to. And you said *it's okay, it wasn't you, just
I had to tell someone.* Because you no longer
write symphonies. The instrument collects dust in
your closet – *where's the music?* We ask. You

answer: *inside, swelling. If there's one thing
you must hear, she will be a cadenza.*

James Croal Jackson

84

Dear Vincent, #15

The Night Café, 1888

They said I'd find you here in the night cafe, that you lived near and here you pass the time. I'm disappointed to find you in this sad place, with its tawdry decor, thrown, not planned. Bleak reds and greens, harsh brights against shadow: truly, wouldn't celibacy be more fun? I've been in similar places before, in bars from Tijuana to Olongapo and Tangiers, doorways in Seville, all smelling of spilled liquor and piss. I find the same folks are here, as I found them there, silent amid the din of inner noise.

Flowers fade in gathering dark
Waiter waits for uncertain train
Clock still reads half-beyond midnight
Well past time to have gone on home.

Kendall Johnson

Dear Vincent, #27

Enclosed Field with Young Wheat and Rising Sun, 1889

I've just read a paper by a psychoanalyst explaining why you juxtaposed complementary colors. They say that it was an expression of your need to synthesize opposites into a whole. And all this time I thought it was to make the colors pop! It seems as if we all look at the world through theoretical glasses. Some write off your devotion to your painting as an obsession that was driven by illness or by shortcomings in your personality. I don't think so. Sometimes, perhaps usually, it takes singularity of purpose, a driving vision – however imperfectly formed that may be – to provide the strength to overcome the voices from without and within that caution moderation and sow self-doubt.

Up early again.
Ate a bit, had some coffee;
shouldered my canvas.
Cypress reaches toward the sky,
wanting to catch the first light.

Kendall Johnson

St. Gertrude Stein

So we go and go until we can't. Then we are there, even if no
    one else is.
There is a stopping point. The view is fixed, stays fixed as long
    as at rest.

Some days we go along out of habit, because we can. It is what
    we do when we
Think of nothing else. One way seems the only way surely as the
    world is round.

And yet, tenderness is an always wish. Shirt left open with living
    underneath.
Buttons, maybe broken. Sun's summer light whenever there is
    summer enough.

This is the way things happen when they happen, which is not
    always. We know
Ourselves only sometimes. And trivia takes up the rest.
    Sometimes, especially.

If there's a loss it's in the leaving. It is in the fast walk or slow
    walk away.
It is in little else, except maybe in a last wave or, more formally,
    a last bow.

Mike James

St. Keith Haring

Imagine you're dancing with a black magic marker. Put your ass
     in the air!
Sniff away at that magic marker smell. Wave at your shadow,
     there to trace.

Gravity loves paint, the way it drips. Red is like blood, can be
     dirty. Those infections.
Sneeze and a whole room gets sick. Cover your mouth when you
     cough. It's your art.

If the day starts yellow in the east, it might stay that way. Hello,
     yellow cat, yellow daisy.
Here's a can of yellow spray paint beside a red wheel barrow.
     What's next? Decisions.

Mornings when all we want is to toss our favorite white coffee
     cup off any rooftop.
Then repeat with another cup. Go on until, outside of baking
     soda, cabinets are empty.

Some images we use just once. Not like that memory of your ass
     in the air!
Most days don't hint at transcendence. We mark time before we
     disappear.

Mike James

Unfinished Poem

for Larry Levis

Here are desires, cave deep
Here is the man and woman who kiss secrets on your bed,
While every light burns in the house
Here is the dream of the butterfly tattoo
and the red shoe box of letters
Here is dust shaken off as an offering on your doorstep
Here is part of the river you always carry
Here is one piece to a child's puzzle
The puzzle piece resembles a mountain or an ocean seen far off
Here is the sound of skipping rope
Here are dandelions, fresh from the ditch's edge

Mike James

What Mattered Most

Standing quietly alone
I watched
as my 5th-grade teacher
Miss Goldwasser
gushed on and on about me
to Mom

My modestly nodding
glowing young Mom

Who wished me
pleasant dreams nightly

Called me Tadeuszu

Mornings served
crunchy warm French toast

Who
after my hospitalization
for surgery to excise
crippling rectal cysts
wiped my 7-year-old butt

Made sure I never wore
hand-me-downs

Protected me from hexes

And who was dead
before I reached puberty
My loving and gentle Mom

Who survived Stalin's Siberia
only to marry The Curse
whose seed gave rise to me

                    And I'd like to say
her happiness
at that parent-teacher meeting
even then

mattered more to me
than my puffed-up chest

But I'd be lying

Ted Jonathan

Old Man Blues

used to be
an over-the-door
mirror
was a comfort

Nowadays
I no longer
own one

& when I pass
the small
mirror that hangs
in my foyer

take
no more
than a quick
sideways glance

never failing
to give myself
the finger

Ted Jonathan

Whisper to a Scream

When the teacher, Miss Eaton, coyly
asked, "On what is our monetary system
based?" we in that six-grade class
sensed that the obvious answer gold
was not the one she wanted. Unraised
hands and silence … But you, Holtz,
whispering *trust* from back of the room,
rang true. And though I was born
knowing that acting too cool to raise
one's hand was foolish, trust, was a thing
this son of chaos wouldn't know.

Last night, a dream: the two of us, Holtz,
a strange basement, and a lone gangster,
his eyes coal-black dots, set to plunge
a dagger he grips two-handed overhead
through your upper back, spots me watching
and runs away, you then vanish, and I,
marked for death, am on the run, desperate
to escape this neighborhood, not knowing
any shortcuts or hideaways, caught by three
gangsters, trying to convince them that I'm
not the outsider for whom they're searching.
But you, who, long ago, whispered *trust*
reappear to betray me – A girl screams –

And I wake to a memory: my little sister
in the shower, water suddenly turned scalding,
and me, believing that our father wasn't
the menace, but the rescuer.

Ted Jonathan

93

No Sign of a Tumor

"You gotta a nice dick," she says. Well alright!
But nice? The way she says it, I know she means
nice like you say after watching your favorite
baseball team turn a dazzling double play. Or how
I felt when I saw my grating next door neighbor's
cockatoo fly out the window. This one, she's blunt,
a tough little nut, but I've got to ... "Big enough?"
"Just right," she says. And she knows dicks. *Just
right.* Two syllables. Syllable for syllable, beating
the six uttered by the doctor years later after yet
another surgery.

Ted Jonathan

Jazz Sequins

and sometimes
there were birds
singing at the night
birds on poles, doin' tin time

wires across the sky
carrying music
equalizer waves
ocean ripples
berries of treasure
a stem to tie the currants
to earth's axis
spinning tunes
as dreamers do

there is a blue jazz beat
a rhythm of river hearts
a flowing aorta of star sprays
in our solar plexus

and we have composed
every song that was ever written
simply by hearing it

and they sent you away
you, who loved the hills and meadows
banging in your head
they said
that you said
there were singular moons
and they said you were crazy

and very late in the evenings
where junkies and protests

are the remotest problems of the universe
and the only task should be
on our dream minds
what happens when people die?
energy is never lost
just subtracted and changed
buried in symmetry

Gloria Keeley

Cold Oven

tires on gravel
the couple drives away
embarking on their travels

hiding behind a rose bush
I leave a rose at their door

I take over their house
I sleep in their bed
I cook on their stove
I wash my clothes in
their machine
cold sheets blow on the line

friends receive my new
phone number
my driver's license has a new
address
mail arrives daily

I walk the invisible dog
to the beach every day
shorebirds search the shore
I give them sand dollars
to purchase the moon
squid prefer clean water
their ink writes chanties
on the ocean floor
terns turn in
five directions
sewing up the points of stars

back home I turn on the oven
the potatoes burn

like hot horses
after a rough night ride
I eat juicy tomatoes
picked from the field
row upon row of
red sea shell souls

the radio news is on
there's a wind over Kansas
rain makes progress
on the roof
the shutters shuffle noisily

I enjoy the evening
beauty salon magazines
on the coffee table
the Braille of piano rolls
etch audio notations

a photo album contains
one baby picture
beautiful rosy cheeks
and dress to match

before bed I go outside
to view the stars and moon
over the house
with my face skyward I
name each constellation

at peace I start back
toward the door
I spot a cross
out farther in the yard
the oven turned off and cold

Here Lies Tiny Alice
her rose dress
emptying in the ground

Undercurrent

from the bed
seaweed dripped from her limbs
salt-licked for succor
the hook, pried from her throat
dropped atop whitecaps

the grey waves slashed the sand
scales fell from her sides;
pieces of moon on the sea

knifed from throat to tail fin
her spine gently lifted from center

after death
shells on stretch of beach
resound the ocean's roar
against her whiteness, her grace

Gloria Keeley

Note to Future Self

You'll come to the day split-knuckled
from the season,
a sky blushing like a secret crush
and all your thoughts, awash as the cloud
of turned up dust from rusted trucks
that pass too loud.
Much has changed.
Your old life cast off like snake skin, where
what remains becomes warmth for birds,
treasure for some 8-year-old boxed
under bed amidst deer bones and odd colored stones.
Everything becomes an artifact.
And because there is a hidden part of the world
that spins some hearty magic –
watch where you step. You'll find these
snakes plainly waiting your bare feet
like some holy ghosts, bidding
a new direction. Do not disparage.
When the woodpecker offers itself to your window
someone new will not be far.
And when those jet trails form a perfect X
across the mark of dusk as you happen upon
your favorite stretch of grass in your yard,
the omen is a good one.
This life is stamped with memos, dispatched
from hidden places exactly when it should.

Casey Knott

Holden Caufield

I lost a brother and a father
In a three-year period
So I understand ...

Some would dismiss your
Story as a long winded rant
After all, artists only name the disease
We don't cure it!

But isn't just naming it enough?

I could never lie as well as you
No matter how hard I try
But fake news could be our reality
Maybe you could take a selfie
And chronicle our decline?

You can tell a lot about a country
By its ruler

Maybe I put too much faith in books

Though I'd rather have words comfort
Me, than fortune or fame
Those are just silly dreams, we
Have, in moments of youthful
Exuberance

I hate phoniness just like you, Holden
But women get boob and butt
Implants
Men become hair club members and
The rich pay hackers to get

Their kids into
College
We can break hearts online
From anywhere in the world
And even a 50,000 a year job
Won't keep us from sleeping
In our cars

The Middle Class is dead;
It's just rich people and everybody else

Once, I wanted a happy life
But now I'll settle for meaningful ...

I'd rather die at 60, knowing I
Lived a life that mattered
Than live to be 90, reveling
In mediocrity ...

They say it all comes down to choices;
But God always has the last word.

I don't even care about getting published
In the *New Yorker* any more
I was a good writer without it,
And it won't make people love me
More

I stopped explaining myself to
People years ago
It hardly matters now, some people
Won't get me, no matter what

As long as I'm happy, that's all
I need

The next time I'm in NYC,
I'll walk down 5th avenue
By Central Park, imagining
Van Morrison's "Moondance,"
As my soundtrack, playing behind me

If a girl smiles at me,
I'll treasure it like a Pulitzer prize
There is no safe place:

But be brave and live anyway

Life is not fair or unfair, Holden
Life just is ...

Erren Geraud Kelly

Always a Deadline
in memory of Beverly Brown

She attended one of my first papermaking workshops
spotlighting the studio like a small sun at high noon
The only one to bring pressed flowers and foliage
from her garden to embellish her papers
And to share the carry-on-suitcase-size box
after which she left the remains for my own use
The same ritual over years
every time she re-enrolled in the class

Always a smile that could
put the bubbles in Champagne
A party that just arrived with all of us
as guests of honor
Her juggling act of career, travel and cat stories
The music and rich tones of voice
when she mentioned her man
Her slow papermaking dance that would
gift one-of-a-kind calligraphied Christmas cards

It had been a long time since I taught
She always at the top of the list for the next class
Maybe a polite call from her occasionally to ask *When*
My answer always *Another deadline to meet first*
One colliding with the next
but promises involving the word *soon*

The final deadline came and went unmet
in the brief days death took to smother
this ball of fire named Bev
Even now her celestial rays cast light
on the shadows of procrastination and guilt
that darken the vats of paper pulp

Ellaraine Lockie

Big Daddy's Dick Burger

It's lunch as apology. The Editor, who goes by The Reverend, says, "I'll take you to my favorite restaurant."

"That won't correct the quote that 'I'd like to have sex with a dwarf,'" says I, who have nothing against dwarves but don't especially lust after them.

"Oh no worries," he says, "I'll publish a disclaimer in the next issue. I'll say, 'She definitely doesn't want to have sex with a dwarf' ... just kidding."

"Well, why not a free lunch." Not that I care what his readers think. I grew up under the microscope of a small farm town. If I hadn't learned to turn off the gossip spigot, I'd have drowned in the rainwater of words.

Mostly trucks sit in front of Big Daddy's Burgers. A trailer house shell in the bowels of Los Angeles. Internal organs of refrigerator, stacks of dishes, hamburger buns, cast-iron grill and bar seats that swivel. Behind the one long counter stands Big Daddy. Built like a brick outhouse. The epitome of a butcher with huge hands flapping over a white apron. Hanging counter-level from an apron dangles a rubber dildo the size of an English cucumber.

"Big Buns Tri Burger, comin' up," he says to The Reverend. "And you," he says, taking a dissecting look at me, "will have a Relish Burger."

"What is it?" I ask.

An indignant voice says, "Burger with relish and mayo."

I can see we're not getting off on the right foot, but I care as much about that as I do about gossip. "I'd like a menu please."

"No menus. I do the ordering," he says.

To which I reply, "But I don't like mayo. I want a cheeseburger with catsup."

"Just scrape it off," he retaliates.

By this time, I'm staring cleavers at The Reverend, who shrugs in that don't-look-at-me, I-didn't-say-it way. I would have pre-ferred the dwarf reputation.

The truck driver sitting on the other side of me swallows a smile when I ask him what he's been force-fed. "A Slab It to Me," he says, before taking the next bite of a burger stacked with bacon, ham and sausage slices. On the other side of The Reverend, the guy asks Big Daddy if Mandy is available.

Big Daddy says, "Was earlier. Left with Hank. Should be about twenty minutes."

The man nudges The Reverend and says to me, "Mandy always gets a Burger Over Easy."

The Reverend leans in and whispers, "They're just having fun with you."

Big Daddy plops our plates down. Along with the dildo that slaps the counter and lays there like a dead pink snake. The plate apologizes with a cheeseburger covered in catsup.

Ellaraine Lockie

Question for Emily Post

He plops a cup holding a red rose
on my Starbucks table
To make your day a little brighter he says
I inhale the rosiest aroma
since my grandmother's garden
Forgetting her adage that every gift has a price
I say *You didn't get this from some drugstore*
It smells delicious enough to be a tea
Says he picked it on the walk from his group home

The poem I'm writing
muzzles my words beyond *Thank you*
Are you a teacher he asks
pointing to pen and paper
No, a writer who comes here to work
What do you write he continues
and reaches for a chair
Eyes and hands return to my tools
while listing four genres
He leaves on cue

Returns with a cup of hot water
containing another rose
You said you wanted rose tea he announces
I don't drink tea and it probably has pesticides
I reply and hand it back
I thought I'd talk to you about writing
I've always wanted to write he says
Pushing the words as hard
as the chair before he drops into it

I tell him *I come here to work*
He sharpens the point of an apology
Pulls another stolen rose

107

from the raped bush out of his bag
Presents it to a woman at the next table

Another man two feet in front of us
bends to pick up a napkin
A four inch butt crack flashes penance
For whom is the question

Ellaraine Lockie

excerpt from The Cyberiad

[Trurl, the constructor, has built Elektrybałt, a machine that could write poems. The machine was given an assignment:]

– Compose a poem about cyberseduction! No more than six lines; in those about love and betrayal, music, blacks, high society, misfortune, incest; cleverly rhyming, and each word beginning with the letter C!!

(...)

Cyprian Cyberseducer

Cyprian cyberseducer, cajoles cynically, cleverly
Countess Charlene's charming carbon-color cheeks.
Continues cittern caresses, chivalry. Calmless Charlene
constantly camouflages consenting, cravings ...
... Calamity comes: Cyprian's cheating – changes course,
caresses closest cousin's captivating calves. Catastrophe!

Stanislaw Lem

translated by Danuta E. Kosk-Kosicka

for mariam

birds of peace and
birds of war and birds
that don't give a shit
anymore.

people playing people
on the sides of a star in
the movies and in the bars
people hanging on and

people hanging out and
people that don't give a shit
anymore
i have no doubt.

we were wild once and clean
as fuck we were dirty but our teeth
were good in other words we
believed we wanted it man
all of it and never let it

stop
and that's exactly what we got
holding hands in the zoo wondering
who's looking at who and honestly

i couldn't tell ya.

Anthony Lucero

another one for mariam

the magic deer wears a
ten foot flame for a coat.
the magic deer slips her
tongue in your mouth. the
magic deer slides her
tongue down your throat.
walking down gardiner
tonight, humid as hell, a
little miniature cow in the
middle of someone's lawn,
surrounded by fireflies, sort
of sums it all up. the world is
going to pot and there's
absolutely nothing you can
do about it. absolutely nothing
you'd want to. i neither love or
understand human beings
anymore, even being one of
them. it's a funny thing to say
but i believe it so it's the truth.
the magic deer makes you whole
and then destroys you. we walk
a little more, say thoughtless
things, then turn back to write
a poem. the magic deer always
goes for the heart.

Anthony Lucero

on the way to albany

on the way to albany we stop at target to get a
mattress cover and pee. i follow a younger
mexican guy into the bathroom and approach the
shortest urinal i've ever seen. he's already in
a stall ass belching, seemingly without shame, while
i struggle to untie the cord on my corduroy pants
which has somehow become a knot, finally unzipping
and springing towards urinary ecstasy. the mexican
guy has gone strangely quiet while i continue to piss. i
imagine him listening to me silently moan in relief.
the red plastic pee hole cover says STRONG MAN
on it with a smiling man making a big muscle of his bicep
in between. that's an odd name for a pee hole cover
company i think, still peeing, but no more odd than the
height of the urinal. it seems to be designed for infants,
and i'm impressed i can still read the branding below.
i leave the mexican guy in silence and tie my pants on my
way out of the store. mariam is in the car waiting with a
mattress cover (wrong size we will later find out) and
happy for she too has peed. we carry on to albany
without fanfare. very little makes sense to me anymore.
it made little sense before but now even the little sense it once
made makes no sense. even wanting it to make sense has
faded. random and reckless temple called it long ago. who
names their kid temple? you can never stop wondering, even
if you do. i was on a plane that seemed likely to crash once.
most everyone on it was acting as you'd expect them to act ...
fainting, praying, screaming, that kind of thing. the girl to
my left was watching a movie without a hint of fear or even
awareness. i spent the better part of what i thought was my
remaining earth time watching her, transfixed. why is she not
acknowledging the flight attendant on her belly in the aisle,
the food and drinks being tossed about, the clear panic of her
fellow passengers? how is she managing it? what drug, what

wisdom, what detachment does this girl possess that we mortals do not? i still think about her on occasion, almost 20 years later now. i would love to talk with her, maybe not talk, maybe just watch a movie, be there with her, regardless of what's happening, just be there with her, watching a movie, enjoying this last little bit.

Anthony Lucero

When Death is a Red Balloon

Scared shitless last week when I
came to your room, saw you asleep
and kept calling your name
pulling your hand, *wake up*, I shouted
until you opened your eyes ...

Oh, I tried again, sat by your bed for hours
holding your hand, sending my voice like a rope
to where you lay several levels below sleep

love, which never made it into word,
flowed through my touch with the meds from IVs
that kept you breathing

and then I saw that red balloon
like those in comics, instead of words,
a wire scrawl of hieroglyphics,
once there, wouldn't go away

I didn't want to see it hovering
near you, but I did; how you'd hate it,
It's not funny, you'd say, blaming me
for what I couldn't control

I watched the air slowly being let out.
Three hours passed and I left ... it was just before ...

the balloon is gone now
you are asleep, I am by your bedside
once again, holding your hand

if you can hear me, I must tell you
there is nothing I can ever imagine experiencing
more horrible than watching the air go out
of that balloon

Linda Lerner

The First Time of Anything

"A British astronaut, Tim Peake, at an outer space station, accidentally misdials a woman, asking, 'Is this planet Earth?' taken as a hoax." – *The Telegraph*

Calendars begin arriving months before
like subway preachers …
he's coming one yells out on an A train,
when? Oct. 25th a voice answers;
he could have said Jan. 1st, as
expectations mount for what
everyone's been waiting for:
not me. A non-believer,

I want an old new year
one that fell out of the sky
like a meteorite, wasn't programmed,
the first time gravity didn't hold me down
and I flew on words, on music
in a ballet class, first time
undressed past skin I flew out
of my body in a man's arms,
stood up naked before a crowd
not caring what anyone thought,
the day my sick cat showed me what
being a mother feels like

each time I flew off the planet
I was raised on, a new year

Linda Lerner

The Professor's Daughter

She drew carefully in the margins
of her notes – elaborate vines,
leaves, flowers. She was quiet,
childlike, sad for all things young
and innocent. Her father made a big
deal about us, explained the literary
genres that our movies belonged to,
kissed our hands like a continental
gentleman. I didn't understand
my friend's disgust. He was so
sweet! *He drinks champagne all day*
was all she'd say. Once she was
in the hospital for three days,
swallowed a bottle of sleeping pills,
but it didn't work. When I felt down,
a shower or a walk were all I needed.
If she had told me the truth
about what her father did to her,
I would not have understood.
My own father drank scotch
and hooted like an owl; nothing
to hold against a man.

Tamara Madison

High School

The first day of school
I was forced to wear a name tag

it read: *hard to pronounce*
my classmates asked me my nationality –

when I said Armenian
they looked like I had insulted their mothers –

where's Armenia, they asked
It's buried in Turkish soil, I replied,

in unmarked graves and river bottoms,
in schools and churches burned to the ground.

The next day, my teachers
invented new names for me

trying on a different one
in each class –

when anyone
asked me my name

I said *call me Brad;*
I'm Irish, German, Dutch and French

my grandparents died in the war –
my classmates smile

and rely on me
to be just like them

anonymous and easy
to introduce to their parents

this is Brad, they say
he's the new kid, isn't he cute.

Michael Minassian

Forever

A road they say few travel, but everyone visits, they buy it,
maybe read a third, talk about it on Facebook. Click and

click again, creating shallow grooves in cyberspace, electrical
impulses that hurt your head. Ventured so far down the oft commented

upon road before they turned around when pavement turned to mud.
"Isn't it romantic? Isn't it sad?" Oh, the world, the world,

these travelers lament.
But they know nothing of this world. Who does?

We skim around on cyberspace, forget our memories. Attention
held for five seconds

phone pings, email rings before we grab a headline,
or dinner. Scan a tweet. When

was the last time we followed something to its end? A friendship?
The dog who lived 14 years, the cat who lived 20? My mother

who went ahead and died after our telephone conversation, before I
could find funds, manage a continent, an ocean and Greenland to
     get to her?

When was the last time you allowed yourself to be carved
sculpted by tectonic plates, weight of a glacier God

stayed present to the slip-strike of geological time
sung through by an ancient voice, kept breathing

stayed in wonder as you became a hollow bone
walking that dubious oft talked about road, changed – irrevocably

Lisa-Marguerite Mora

Wolf

giving you the format, Jack – Guru

Wolf was a surveyor
a *coureur des bois*
observing the frontier
but unlike Tocqueville
she was no visitor

The American
never Wolf's friend
eventually was persuaded
to give her Yellowstone
but there was a catch

A National Park
it would do double duty
as a trophy garden/taxidermy stop
to draw tourists and pay for itself

We, the People don't really mind
Wolf getting her share
it's just her tendency to still wear fur
proving she's a queen on welfare

Romulus & Remus insist
they are not Wolf's children
simply present for jury selection
mistaken for family relations

Turkey was going to be our national bird
but we were scared and settled on a raptor.

Jeremy Nathan Marks

Face Transplant

for Katie Stubblefield

Nobody wants to be the weird woman
who shot off her face.

Nobody wants to be scorned,
forgotten, live the death
of whoever she was, walking
a path to nowhere,
singing a plaintiff song,
its trombones
sliding across time.

Nobody wants to kill
just her face. She wants
to murder her whole body,
still her heart,
be a corpse, not a living frame
with a head-rage
where love got buried
in blood and bullets.

I got a new face
to fill the void, new lips
blistered by the west wind
eyes the color of grief,
nose that can almost smell
the past when I thought
he might still love me.

I never imagined doctors
lining up
to sew new skin,
gristle and bone,

bringing my scars back to life
under the knife.

It wasn't what I expected,
not at all, when I stuck
the rifle under my chin
and pulled the trigger.

I wanted to be
the abandoned lover
who died to be remembered,
kissed in the coffin,
shrouded in
muslin and lace,
a bride, married
to the idea of marriage,
laid out in silver slippers.

Linda Neal

Great, Again?

To make the country great again
He made the country hate again
And hell and horror, history –
Calm down, I'm talking *Germany*.

James B. Nicola

North Gable

While I was lying in the house alone
last night, the gable door bulked open
by itself, and in the darkness I
could see into the Small Unknown, by day
a bare wood floor swept schoolhouse clean,
a storage bin for useless things, like
Mom and Dad's old luggage (on their last
long journey, they took nothing with them);
my dead sister's knitted sweaters left
from high school. "Why do I linger here?"
I wondered half out loud, "while all I've loved
(though just a mile or so down-road)
is infinite years from sight,
is a stone city with only stars for light?

William L. Norine

Sedentary

It's not the industrial age
anymore but we like tradition

too much – pledging allegiance,
apple pie, hard labor –

America. We commute
ourselves to office chairs, glue

our eyes to blue light screens,
hold our breath and count to 8.

We wear our back pain to bed,
wake up, and do it again

while the kids grow up on Diet Coke
and balloon like mortgages.

Our pants are adjusted for inflation,
our salaries are sedentary,

and we're doing just fine
hanging on by a single bootstrap.

Kendra Nuttall

Satan's Snowball

(For Howard Finster, Man of Flame and Visions)

Let me explain the facts of the truth.
I have been called crazy just for you.
You can have a helluva time
if you don't mind smoke and fire.
You can smoke without your pipe.
I am a man of many visions.
I am the world's red light.
I will cover the world in ministering.

If a man's soul
wears gospel shoes,
he shall walk
over the pinpoint
of the devil's pitchfork.
A man lives in his shoes a long time.
His shoes save his feet from
the devil's gravel.
If yee shall fall, don't whimper.
If yee shall smell the dread sulphur,
shake your head.
If yee shall get stepped on,
be up. Keep walking.

If you don't walk with the gospel,
you won't have to waste time drinking water.
You won't need a pitchfork,
that's the devil's job.
You will enter a fiercy whorl.
You will become a serpent of the wilderness.
You will become a sniffer, a fly flap,
You will become Satan's snowball.

Suzanne O'Connell

A Woman Shall Compass a Man
(For Howard Finster, A Stranger From Another World)

I painted on a woman's shoe once.
Of course, her foot
was not in it at the time.
I had no thirst for women.

Pauline was sweet on me when we met.
I had no idea.
She was fourteen,
we often walked to church.
One Sunday she gave me her school picture.
I put it in my billfold.
Don't get me wrong,
she was okay,
but my mind was on
ministering the Many Mansions.
I knew that women could bring fever,
and fever would bring torment in hell.

I painted Marilyn Monroe's picture once.
Her dress was the devil's job,
showing the tops of her flesh parts.
I painted my face right there,
above her parts.
Below my face, in the crack,
I painted the devil.

I forgot to mention,
I looked at Pauline's school picture
years after she gave it.
I said to myself:
This is my one woman.
If she shall not have me,
I will have no other.

We had us five children.
After five children,
Pauline was wore out.
This was in nineteen and fifty four,
around when I painted Marilyn.
I wrote on it:
Stars Are Great by Howard Finster,
Sent To You All.

Suzanne O'Connell

Tying Flies

Rain froze on the driveway
late this afternoon. I'd come home
early for my four o'clock nap.
The trash containers were still
on the curb so I thought I should
pull them up into the garage.
I slipped on the new ice
but only briefly, since it was
patchy, the cold not having
deepened. There was mail
in the mailbox, all bills or junk
advertisements. I wadded them
into my coat pocket and started
up the slippery slope. The tree
beside the house, an ornamental
of some type, was scraping the paint
in the steady wind, fingers
clicking against the wallboard.
I thought of my brother, back
when he was smaller than me,
hunched over his desk, squinting
at the flies he was tying. Neither
of us ever fished for anything more
than perch. I hadn't remembered
the bottle-blues in years, the
small feathers, or the hook eyes.
I guess it was my brother's long fingers,
his small rounded shoulders,
practicing, as I teased, for old age,
the rain turning in the cold
to the ice we fear.

Al Ortolani

*

To listen you work this bowl
and each evening crouch
with your lips in all directions

wrapped around a warming spoon
near, nearer to the side she slept on
filled with sharp corners

and lower your forehead, let the soup
cool – you swallow a bed, are fed
on windswept fires, the sound

that has become the mouth
you're drowning in – arm over arm
making room for her and lower.

Simon Perchik

*

This battered window box
has found an opening
– with a single flower

is taking on the sun
though you use well water
fitting it into its shadow

as if madness needs a corner
for its darkness reaching out
he way your heart was filled

with river noise
that has nothing left to give
– what you hear is the sun

swallowing ice as the antidote
to flower after flower and the mist
from someone breathing.

Simon Perchik

*

With the door gone now
you set out for the waterlogged
as if some makeshift plank

could face shore as a stone
already upright, filled
with branches and salt

though there's no sail
and even more than the sea
you have no place to mourn

– you need driftwood :a mask
held in place by an emptiness
certain it arrived before you.

Simon Perchik

Waking with the Muse

She cracks the dawn in half
and releases the sun.

Gold pours through black leaves,
sparking them jade.

I look inside morning's shell
to a moment no one has seen –

no lip prints of words
to smudge the air,

no leftover regret dragging
its shadow to the shoreline.

A ginkgo, still flaming,
sets loose its egret,

as gilded white silence
skims the lake.

Patty Dickson Pieczka

Shape Shifter Muse

On moss-strewn mornings like this,
clouds shading the pergola, she
shows me how to speak without words.

Her voice drifts from the mouth
of a spoonbill, a snake's rattle,
a creaky wooden rowboat.

She knows my thoughts
are circling but cannot land,

yet they perch on her arm
like white doves on an oak limb.

She is the old stone cottage
filled with ghosts, the spell
drifting through misty

bayou palmettos,
the love charm found
in a dusty attic chest.

She is there when time sleeps
through its lazy hours

and the hallway clock
ticks backward.

Patty Dickson Pieczka

Why?

Because a body is still a body, until it breaks.

And even then, it will find its way to laughter.

Because your lungs will ultimately accept whatever you breathe into them.

Because your mother is still your mother until one of you forgets your own shadow.

Because you were born upon your mother's bones, and every time you dream,
       you return to those closed walls,
              you return to your mother.

Why?

Because, if only for one night, Johanna, may you be made holy. If only for one breath, may you be allowed to pray to your God.

Where has your God gone now? After all this time, was He just another word for Mother?

Is that what was meant by all those men, with their chains and their commandments?

God, nothing more than a mistaken pronunciation that slipped off the root of some soldier's tongue.

We already know that if God were to exist at all, she would take the form of your mother.

Why?

Because this body was born tired. It bleeds in silence.
Because this body is only 21 years old, yet it has already found
its home within the mouth of a river.
This body, which one day, will once again be made into a rock
within the water. Sinking, only to survive.
Dying, only to breathe.

What peace there is within that truth.

Why?

Because this boy is still just a boy, no matter what he claims, no
matter how hard he prays not to be. His spine is still made up of
his mother's wings, and when he surrenders to it, he swears that
he is flying.

I am sorry, Johanna. Sorry that I did not seek forgiveness sooner.

Johanna, when will we both understand, that there is nowhere
else for us to dream ourselves, except back into our mother's
chests? Our bones, their bones, our names just other words for
beauty. Our mothers, the first Gods, to grant us beauty at all, Johanna.

I love you, Johanna, but apparently not enough to stay. Apparently not enough to live by what I preach. I love you the way a
boy loves the horizon his father made for him, knowing he will
never reach it, nor his father. Knowing that the possibility of
transcending the both of them is soothing enough. What would
he even do once he caught it? I hope he never knows the answer.

Why? Should I tell you why, Johanna?

Because these bodies are not clean, nor are they good. Because we learned how to hurt first, then ask forgiveness. Because, we are children who will always shed our skins in search of new visions, and we wore one another so proudly, for so long. It was only fitting that we ended up at the bottom of a river.

Why? Can I finally tell you why, Johanna?

Because when I dream, I feel myself return to you.
And in that space, where we are separated from everything we have been taught,
Where the only indicator of time is some broken alarm in the far-off corner of another room,
We can finally begin the process of teaching one another,
How for the first time,
to spell out the word "mercy,"
in the dark.

Ian Powell-Palm

I Wish William Burroughs was My Mother

We gathered at the café to celebrate William Burroughs'
104th birthday, poets and writers, artists and lovers, all
hailing the junk master, the gun-toting queer loving naked
razor of a cadaver, inventor of the phrase "heavy metal,"
owner of a dildo christened "Steely Dan." Anne Waldman
chanted, Aimee Herman cut-up, Jan Herman remembered,
Penny Arcade shared with us bits of Burroughs' axioms,
his words of advice to young people. *Avoid fuck-ups,* he
counseled, *or you will be a fuck-up, too. Don't talk to the
mentally ill,* cautioned Bill. *They will only make you crazy.*
Awed by his practicality and pragmatism, I found myself
wishing that William Burroughs was my mother. I doubt
that my unruly hair or ripped jeans would have driven him
to lie in bed, kicking his pasty white legs and threatening
suicide. If he'd discovered my secret pot stash, he surely
would have smoked it up himself, and lied about it, but I
don't think he'd have threatened me with lifetime lock-up
in Kings County for possession of it, or kicked me down
the stairs for coming home at 4AM from the Fillmore East.
More than likely, he would have been out himself, engaged in
activities both interesting and illegal, and much too busy to
care about my bad grades, lame love letters, and Parliament
cigarettes. I'm sure that his son, poor Willie, Jr., if he'd lived,
would disagree with me about his parental worth, but allow
me to be quite clear: I do not wish that he had been my father.
I wish that William Burroughs was my mother – unemotional,
sensible, detached, disdainful of the stupid and the crazy,
playing Three Card Monte with the devil, who is no more
or less dishonorable than the priest. *They all cheat,* he would
have warned me, *and anyone who says they aren't in it for
the money is in it for the money.* I hope my pretend Mother
is having himself a happy one hundred and four, that he's
writing another novel just to keep busy, keeping an eye out
for old junk pushers dropping dollars on the ground, and Him
in his black hat, always careful about whose money he picks up.

Puma Perl

139

Both Hands

Because I get along with myself, I've never been accused of mistaken identity. Yesterday, me and Cricket drank some food-flavored vodka. It was clear as morning light, and tasted like Iowa top soil. She said *It won't hurt you Dale, if you drink it fast.* This is a nice little town. The buildings are square; not too tall, not too short. First impressions are so important. Cammo Ricky walked by and said we should go over to the Dollar Store sometime, but Cricket and Cammo don't get along, so, me and Cricket hung back on Lafayette, between 7th and 9th. I remember one day Cammo said, Dale, *when you die, a few people remember you. Then they die. So, you'd better build yourself a pretty big pyramid.* Cammo went to college. Since Iraq, he's had a little trouble now and then. Gets along fine with animals, but doesn't like people much. I guess even a veteran farmer still needs both his hands.

Brad Rose

The First Juror Receives a Visit

Your house is quiet.
It's a good neighborhood.
The afternoon light, fall-sharp as it stabs
through the vertical blinds.
My hair's cut short like Jesus'
that time he ran out of gas in the desert.
Nobody recognized him for who he was.
Not even God.

I've been counting the days since the sentencing;
one thousand eight hundred and thirty.
Most ideas don't last this long.

When you come home, you'll open the front door,
think it's just your husband in the back room,
think he came home early from work.
You'll call his name.

Can hardly wait to see your face again,
innocent as an astonished angel's.
If you don't recognize me,
I'll re-introduce myself,
be glad to show you just how guilty
I really am.

Brad Rose

Lost Home Movies

His smooth, charismatic voice
broke up the static of the collect calls
he sent my mother from
a minimum security federal prison
most days after I got out of school.
He tripped out on the fact that
he created me with his seed.
He also broke the news to me
the night before my tenth birthday
that I'd never be nine years old again,
and that I was closer to the end
of all that we can see or dream.
I was proud to no longer believe
in Santa and the Tooth Fairy,
yet I believed the lies
they all told me of my
father's heroism in an unjust world
that took him away from us.
He charmed my mother long enough
for her to find the good buried inside of him,
before he fooled her for all eternity, and
I'll never have another father to fool me again.

Kevin Ridgeway

Floating on the Pale Backside of Death

One summer after he was paroled,
my father and I decided to fill
our empty swimming pool with
garden hose water. We both
performed handstands in secondhand
swim trunks and talked about
going to Forest Lawn Cemetery
to check out the celebrity graves
that afternoon. We soon
blasted out of the driveway
in his vintage El Camino,
both of us still damp from
jumping off the diving board
and into a shallow sea
of filthy water. We were on
our way to the cocktail party
of dead celebrities, all of them
hidden behind marble
and under the imported grass
of surrounding hillsides.
They were our best friends
because they never talked back
or dared to even judge us,
and they always saved the day
with a glamour that made
us drown in our attempts
to escape from the low-class
prison we found ourselves in
off screen, both of us missing
on the cutting room floor.

Kevin Ridgeway

Jesus Rice

"Didi!" my daughter scolds, using my Grandpa name,
when, unthinking, I let fly
a "fuck" or a "shit" or an "asshole"
in the presence of her two-year-old daughter.

I've always had a potty mouth,
which didn't seem to damage Anna,
a woman who speaks five or six languages,
ranging from French to Urdu.

So, picking them up at the airport,
I curse when a car cuts me off
at the exit, automatic as shifting into gear,
eliciting another "Didi!" from Paloma's mom.

Only, as we continue toward our destination,
from her perch in the carseat in back,
I hear Paloma chirping "cheesy rice!"
like a macaw repeating sounds it's heard.

Charles Rammelkamp

rock 'n' roll and World War I: two meditations

i

Wilfrid Owen, every one of us believes,
never heard Jimi Hendrix's right hand speak.
as certain can we be that Eliot (he)
heard Beatles and others croon late in his years
(their ubiquity a burst exploded shell
their decibels tuned to challenge cannons' roars).

rock 'n' roll could be no echo of world war
unless fidelity to sides One and Two
could be produced and captured: screams of young men

denied to at least two generations born
dead into the air atop pulverized fields.

ii

Zimmerman had not been warned Sandburg was deaf,
this Swede who had no Nobel prize to confer:
to whose memory might Sandburg have been tuned?

Sandburg was equipped with his healthy red ears
just as Guthrie had had his healthy red tongue:
and all three men knew about holding guitars.

could he hear battlefields a century old
the day that Zimmerman auditioned and played?
could Sandburg's reverie have been tuned to war?

after forty years 1918's faint roars
could have intruded for entire quarter-hours.

Edward Burke Roberts

Severance Pay

I return to my car
after a two hour morning walk
along the headlands

I'm parked in a gravel lot
next to the motel
where I worked
when I lived out here
almost 20 years ago

before they fired me
for my youthful inability
to disguise my contempt
for the arrogant prick in charge

I notice my coffee cup's empty
and I think of that place in town
but then I see
the open lobby doors
people milling about inside
having breakfast

"fuck it"

and I go in
looking a bit scruffier
than the other patrons
but the receptionist smiles
and I smile back

then I fill my coffee mug
look around
and wow!

complimentary breakfast
in a 200 dollar a night joint
is a lot better than the stale cornflakes
and bruised bananas
at the 60 dollar dump I'm staying in

so I grab a blueberry muffin
a yogurt from the fridge
a couple of sausage patties ...

and as I go back out the door
I nod to the receptionist
and say "Have a nice day!"

I walk the meadow path
out to that cypress grove
on a cliff facing the sea

I sit on a fallen log
watch the breakers roll in
and chew my severance pay
with a big ol' smile

shit ...
I might just go back tomorrow!

Brian Rihlmann

Thursday Night at the Emergency Department with My Suicidal Client (Who Shall Remain Nameless)

A man's moaning like an old ship
drool spilling onto his threadbare shirt
he slips in front of us
at the admission desk
the staff yell, *Get in line, Gary!*
Gary's legs are broken masts
he shambles back and forth to the patient toilet
in Jesus sandals
a mash-potato of a woman is flanked by security guards
flight-risk cutter, rum-drunk
shushed for screeching
along to her iPod
She fuckin' hates me!
Yeah yeah yeah! on repeat
a female guard asks what song that is
Everclear, Kelly mumbles
and I know she's wrong
but I can't think of who wings it
I have to get through this night
like everyone else
after midnight
I stop perking up like a meerkat
at every person in hospital blue
hoping they're coming for my client
a woman nearby shoulders a blanket
hugging herself
soundless tears salt her cheeks
looking beyond the corridor
beyond the EXIT diagram
into nothingness
there's something about her
that reminds me of myself
my mother
died alone

in the early hours of the morning
she always said, *That's history*
but history repeats
doesn't it, Daughter?
I ask the woman, *Are you in pain?*
(my mother lying on the hospital bed
her head slowly turning towards me
the day before she died)
the woman replies it's in her belly
It's pulsing red
she's from Chile
My husband isn't allowed in here
I tell her he is
she calls him on her phone
we talk, she smiles
we're laughing when he arrives
they just moved up from Hobart
A mistake to come to a big city
she grew up in Santiago though
It will take time, I say
a doctor beckons her behind a blue curtain
kidney infection
she's wheeled away in a bed
grins as she rolls by
doesn't even know my name
maybe someone will be kind to me
when I'm suffering
alone
the guards bring Kelly cups of coffee
Gary waves as he shuffles past.

Maree Reedman

A Landscaped Garden, for the Addict

While I turned the earth upside
down and cut back the juniper's arms,
those dead arteries of wood,
I thought of you
in your late-morning bed of dreams.

I walked around the Japanese maple,
and tried to pick up the thread of light
that dances there sometimes and turns the world
green. I saw desire rising in the hardy fuchsia,
its red bells and crimson half-moons
moving slightly in the breeze,
making morning seem like evening.
The air glittered with overheard telephone conversations
and spiders who amassed their silken avenues,
their chances to connect.

Now I imagine your chin
dropped to your chest, and you
taken in again by the poppy,
every nerve-ending waving in unison
as if to say *it is a far distance to paradise*
but we may yet arrive.

The grass grows ragged around
the little semblance of order I have reclaimed,
how you are brilliant in your craving
for only the heart of the flower,
as you fall further into those sleeves of dark
which the high has bought for itself now,
your life.

Judith Skillman

Miracle

This poem should've died two poems ago,
Should've drowned in water after a lingering
Thunderstorm turned cracked dirt into rushing
Streams of suffocating mud and sharp objects
Unseen. But some things do emerge from
The dead, breathe new life unto themselves
Like the Lord did with Lazarus four days after
His heart stopped pumping blood to the rest of
His sickly body. This wasn't the case with my
Friend Austin, shot more times than I have digits,
Though I wasn't holding my breath. But sometimes,
Miracles do happen, and try as you might, you can't
Deny them even with your eyes and ears shut tight.

Alex Z. Salinas

Homerun

Babe Ruth comes to visit me.
Together we say goodbye
to the bleachers, box seats,
the press box, goodbye
hotdog barker,
to the kids cheering,
the Sunday redhead mother
holding up her baby – for him
stepping up to the plate.
Goodbye World Series,
the pennant waving fans,
spring season, goodbye

summer, goodbye autumn.

Winter Park, nonetheless
the stands packed,
all the diehards
coming to their feet
take off their hats, my turn
at bat, the air gone
icy still. Oh, Babe!
I lift an arm, point with you
to the center field wall.
Follow my eye, follow
the ball, how we are one
sure shot out of the Park.

Martin Steingesser

Toward the End of Everything

I buried your father today
while I was earning my living
I almost say as the young girl embraces me
while I am walking my dog this evening
thanking me for the home-cooked dinner I
drove to her mother's house this evening
and I loved him and will do anything to help you
I murmur in my deep soul-searching voice
because I loved him and we drank together
often and fought against the tyranny of hate
and didn't trust the media but trusted love,
and still I know I buried him too soon
about the time he buried me too beneath it all
while he was still breathing and the media
talked of the economy and baseball and
how many celebrities died or were in scandals
and tried to sell us medicines for forever
under that bombardment of 24-hour news
we talked to the end of secrets we would share
and you were at the heart of his, child,
and I feel your breasts against me briefly
sun setting beyond the mountains before us,
knowing that other things always got in the way
and we trusted each other as the best of friends
while we hid our fear of death from each other
and drank to the many little battles lost or won.
There was too little time. I wrote poems for him
toward the end of everything.

When you have lived as long as we once did
you know the lies about never being able to return home
have a meaning beyond the lies and mistakes we all make,
that the small clearing with the woodland cabin
now half overgrown with weeds and rotted windows
is lost spinning in the time continuum behind us,

that the path may be the same, the initials carved on trees,
but the universe itself has moved on, the space is time
and time itself is lost in the icy darkness of the soul.

And yet we do read the papers. We did too long.
We believed the iron irony of political patriotism
and the virtue of earning a living on the souls of others
while giving out a little to see them through.
And so we died a bit each day. It catches up at least.
I want to tell you this, but an evening walk is too short
and so the words come out on paper wherever paper leads.

When Kim died in Vietnam the stone behind him
was red for twenty days before the rains washed it away.
For twenty years we had shared our dreams and were blind
The Earth was as hungry as the monsters of textbooks.
I tried to visit him at home last Sunday but in the cold
that hung from those rafters was now the Internet
and a GSP that was based in time outside our time.
The family living there now was scared. No dreams.

This was before you were born, but the schools,
the universities you studied in, the corporations
your father and I stood against outside the news
all took their form in that distant universe.
Your eyes and yes your breasts are born of this
and the children that will come will be weaned
on the fights we fought and on the dreams
that even we are indifferent to now
and your children on a distant star will know
it was a long time ago in a space right here.

Jared Smith

Dreams of the Dead

You are not listening.
Trees are doubled over in madness.
The ocean comes at you fiery
throwing shells, seething,
seaweed foaming from its mouth.

Each day we are gunned down
perpetually dying along the beach,
our screams lost among seagulls
our agony echoing in conch shells
where our words are lost in time.

We think we are getting to you,
slowly one day to the next though.
We dream a strategy of making love
to everything you have learned to love,
to bind our broken arms around it
knowing this will draw you to us.

Jared Smith

What He Became

After the car wreck,
after the twenty-eight vehicles of torn metal
blazed into the dark smoke that filled that night
he was lost even as he fell through the doorway
its hinges hanging loose at the edge of the universe,
then slumping from the flashing bubblegum machines.

After the explosion that engulfed that night on I-70
outside Denver he became the fire and fury about him
and dropped through the mangled dreams that bound him
and found himself in his body alone at the edge of the highway
while the media and their helicopters flew on high,
and as the bodies burned he rose into the night
and as the winds passed through him he forgot his name
and the lights were blinding, but he turned away.

After he forgot the name he was given, after that
moment when his reality was ripped open he found
himself pulling back from the smoke choked speedway
assembly line of manufactured dream cash coins
enveloped at first by only darkness as he began to rise
from whatever darkness had lain in wait for him for years
and he no longer heard the voices laying claim,
and as he left the city below him his lungs began to fill
with stars whose names he no longer remembered
and he became the mountains and the night,
his car far too small to contain what he became.

Jared Smith

Wasted Words

A husband sat at his desk late into the night. His lamp shone in a narrow cone as will a star that beams light while conceding blackness all around. He could not write. His wife far away, he could not think of the words that would furl the distance between them like the flag from a divided country. Everything I wrote before was for you, he thought, but now I can't even write you a letter.

Then it occurred to him to write it in urine. He had seen other men writing so in snow, although that struck him as inefficient. Shall I send her a frozen hillside through the post? Will winter follow my words like smoke behind a train? Icicles will droop from the mail sorter's nose. The mailman will need mittens, and then how will he pluck letters from his bag?

I am a man of tradition, and I will use snowy white paper. My yellow words will melt through the crust of its surface.

Quill in hand, he began to write, the blockage broken in the rush of words onto paper. His penmanship flourished, his cursive became crisp and full of grace notes, his syntax grew ornate and passionate. He poured out his feelings onto the page and felt triumph. What fountain pen could be finer? Though the ink is cheap, the words come from deep within.

Yet all too soon, the words ran out; the sentences, for a time so copious, slowed to a trickle.

This is divorce, he thought: a failed correspondence, tortured, alone, holding your penis in the dark, and all your best words wasted.

If You Might Be Dying

In a world dying,
it's unwise to possess sentiment,
pursue an impulsive romance,
or love birds, cats and dogs.
Your fragile part, the heart,
may burst from your chest and risk

flopping on the asphalt at great risk
to you. You'll be dying
and literally heart-
less, thus incapable of sentiment.
That heart is now dessert for dogs
that possess no romance

in their bones, no wish to romance
a cat or a bird or a hydrant without risk-
ing their nature as loyal dogs.
And, friend, if you might be dying,
die without regret, or sentiment,
hold your friend – your heart –

for dear life. Rush to the room where hearts
recover, where you may relearn romance
in spite of the exhausted world, sentimental-
izing what remains left of time. Risk
a memory of your lover dyeing
his hair red, holding you, your two dogs,

hugging them with a wan smile. A dogged
desire to deem the heart
larger than living or dying,
as your lover lives for romance
when he gazes into your eyes, risks
believing that life lacks sentiment.

And as you recall that love, that sentiment,
forget if each of you acted like dogs,
hitting, biting, exposed the other to risk.
Forget the times each of you lacked a heart
to share and that no dreamy, romantic
counselor prevented unavoidable dying

with sentiment. No, hide your tired heart
where dogs can't sniff out the romance
of risk that's unafraid of living or dying.

David Spicer

Leave Me Alone, I was Only Singing

At some point someone discovered
it is easier to destroy than to create,

and that's how it started.

They went and canceled beauty
because it was problematic
on the best of days,

they exiled it to the wasteland
of unsafe spaces.

They gathered up
the poets
and the artists,

both the living
and the dead,

greeted them
with howls
of execration

before extracting
confessions
and apologies

for the harm
they had done
the communities,

and went on to erase
their works and bodies
in solemn ceremony.

They played a concerto
of whatever semblance
of music was still allowed,

to commemorate the occasion,
to usher in the new golden era

in which all bad dreams were banished,
and every good citizen too woke to sleep.

William Taylor Jr.

Come Home, Kevin Spacey

I've been told that Da Vinci kept a twelve year old boy
as his concubine, and that Cellini was a rapist: Celine
an anti-Semite; Pound a fascist; Bukowski a misogynist;
Polanski a pedophile; Rimbaud a slave trader; Genet a thief and
Ben Johnson a murderer.

But I ask – should the sins of the artist overflow, infecting the
art? Should we throw acid in the *Mona Lisa*'s face, burn the can-
tos and jackhammer *Perseus With The Head Of Medusa*?

Perhaps a darkened soul allows embarkment on a *Journey To
The End of the Night.*

We sinners are the creators, especially when haunted by guilt –

The saints have left no artistic legacy, for which we should all
be grateful.

Ron Terranova

162

Answer Me

I still ask, just as I did as a child, only no longer on my knees.

Usually I ask in the shadow of night, or sometimes in the day when there should be shadows, but there are none.

I talk to you, muted, in whispers. "Talk to me – speak, or at least give me a sign – an omen."

We pray, and we beg. We supplicate and sacrifice, and you remain silent as the hours grow desperate and immolation is near.
Is this how it is to be? The silent void, empty and cold, to be filled with madness and anarchy?

The danger is not when we stop believing in you – it is when we still believe, but know we are better than you.

Ron Terranova

Alleys and Parking Lots

I just happened to be there to witness a small cat chasing drifting feathers in a downtown parking lot, too immersed in living to even know he didn't have a home. Debates of well-intentioned mission or vulgar intrusion aside, I pondered a course to follow …

It reminded me of all the lessons I never learned from my father, who gushed that you only help the weak if you are soft, help the abandoned if you are lost, and only feel pain if you're not inflicting it.

His parish was a growling scimitar of rabid dogs, chasing the brightness away from every living corner. Great black-winged birds flooded his stillborn sky, all set on a canvass of simmering rage, its sullen closed-mouth colors forever on the prowl for care-free joy.

A frigid, wind-swept bay of half-light was a safe nursery for the dogs to roam, but ceaseless winters bred only black full moons that no longer commanded echoes of trenchant howling. And so the many passing years softened the beasts, and finally on a warm spring night, they quietly turned down a dank back alley and disappeared.

Letting go of his mad imaginings and his puerile curses was as close to peace as he'd find, and I, witnessing the last shadowed flickers of the light dowsed from him in this air of bleeding dust, was as close to understanding as I would ever know …

And if I had not brought home the rain-sparkled kitten from the downtown parking lot, my soul would not be worth the paper it's bleeding on

Brian K. Turner

Amirah Al Wassif

from Baraka to mother Eve!

Dear and poor Eve,

I am writing to you now without putting my right hand on my
chest, quivering from cold and grief.
I don't cry any more mom, just hide under our destroyed table,
count my breath.
a very long time spent while my humble sitting holding my dirty
cotton doll, watching the footsteps of the hurry passengers on
our crowded road.
As usual, I am putting my mad eyes into the wide openings of
our ragged tent, waiting to catch someone's eyes, perhaps seeing
those eyes convincing me that I am still alive!
I am still your sweet daughter, your lovely baby, the crawler on
the sharp platforms every midnight, I am still your patience girl
who walking after your shadow, looking for the warmth of your
heart and the smell of your face.
last night I dreamed about you, I was showering under the honey
down, and you appeared *obviously in front of me and tried your
best to touch my little belly with your warm fingers, in my* dream,
I was the baby girl with wavy hair and you were my immortal
mother who still moving her big fingers under her baby belly in
order to make her laughing, but in spite of her great job, her baby
still crying!
I am writing to you with a flushed dirty face and unique kind of
delicious confusion which make me whisper through the long
hours of the day and night, whispering like an immigrant bird
which may dissolve because of the thrill of meeting!

it is my dearest confusion, I have ever taken in my whole life as
a woman decided to write with her foot for a long time. everybody here in my world still wondering how could a woman dare
to write with her foot?

165

everybody here in my (third world) whispers from the first light on down until the last light of twilight, my people want seriously to catch my inner secret, they addicted to asking each other about my upturned situation.

"writing with your foot, how dare you?!" they cried in front of my face and behind my back. they never stop asking and asking and asking, and I concealed my heart very well because in the case of they saw it, they will discover immediately my secret, if it happened, they will know the only answer of "how a woman dare writing with her foot?"
my days act her last dance with shaken fingers and bare feet, surrounded with walls, only walls around me, watching me, touching my pain, only walls listening to my forbidden song, only walls witnessing my writing fever,
only these inanimate objects feeling more than living people!
if you are a writer, there will be a weird rumor never leave you which based upon some upper stories such as you use the stars as punctuation, and the blue of skies is your immortal ink that never runs dry, and you have a deal with angels and devils, also you spy on every insect crawled on the earth.
if you are a writer, you may see the shadow of William Shakespeare every midnight above your head, explain to you how to eat the time, how to dissolve yourself between letters, he will explain to you how to put your heart on the paper without pretending.
as a woman decided to write with her foot, I just asked how to think differently, how to play with your imagination ball like a professional player?
my name is Baraka, one of those homeless women who spent their spring age on the cold sidewalks, eating nothing, feeling nothing, tried their best to tame neediness.
I have no idea about the rosy dreams and all I know is scratching the trash cans every night.
And about my pillow, it is not surprising to be a haystack!
When the honey down, watered my hair, I figured out that I am in the middle of nowhere when the headlights blocked my sight, I touched my darkness.

Who am I?
I am a very patient crawler on the rough edges of life, I am a naked woman because of the conspiracy of poverty, lean body stretched along with the torn papers which covered the pavement.

I am here writing in my mind, in my blood, create my own imaginary world which doesn't seem similar to my harsh fate.
all my whole life, I have been covered with an ecstasy of writing.
I gorge my poor flesh with clay and this weird stuff, not my choice at all.
dear Eve, I were dissolving under the furious sky, need your help to clean my dirty body, I am here in one of the street corners recalling your great spirit against the boys who chased me by throwing clay which forced me to run away, in fact, I couldn't escape away from their harsh beats, but really I do it,
literary, I ran away here in my imaginary world!
I have shed tears here under the elder tree, touching my ribs during that much time.
I am not blind, I am just half-educated woman who lives in a separate tent on one side of our hungry street, a half-educated woman who still desperately dreams to finish her education, but how an orphaned female in the third world dares to demand to achieve any dream except getting married?!

I was crawling on the floor, trying to count my breath slowly and hurry. It is my exclusive moment where I stitch my poetry piece. The very last time when I contemplate myself as a baby with a wide mouth and curious eyes.
And the hours pass heavily, my poor heart couldn't bear any more. yes, it is me the funniest creature you see ever, the ocean which walks on two feet, and that idiot elephant which bitterly wishes to fit the crazy fashion

There is a mysterious voice escaping away from the ticking of my watch, the voice haunted me, but my soul with a harsh weapon, here in the heart of my ears all these secrets which nights hide them very well, every secret scream in the silence of space "who am I?" and I join in their mourning now with non-stop of repeating "who am I?!"

Your daughter
Baraka

Blue Karate

now she is walking to me
all our shadow life plays between us
buzzing like dust in a sunbeam.

now she is walking to me
she liked locking eyes hiding hearts
because it flips me over

like Blue Karate

Michael K. White

At the Salon

I hear that Monday is a holiday
election day tomorrow
and that is why
the tricycles with sidecars
paraded last night down the street
last minute electioneering
and that is why
they set off fireworks
and honked their horns
hoping for votes

Paula Yup

Thelma's House

in Eagle Rock
where I lived
before moving
LA to Woods Hole
with Dean
a college friend
throwing my lot with love
gambling my life away

Things We Did

you saved a coral reef
I wrote a book

Paula Yup

৵ Some Particulars ৶

J. Lester Allen is an American writer and poet. Originally hailing from the Central Pennsylvania region, he currently calls the waterfall rich holler of Ludlowville, NY home. He published his first collection of poems, *The Days Carnivore*, in 2008 and has since published three other books, most notably *This Is a Land of Wolves Now* (Kung Fu Treachery, 2019).

Jason Baldinger is from Pittsburgh, PA. He is co-founder and co-director of The Bridge Series. His books include *Everyone's Alone Tonight* (with James Benger) and *The Better Angels of our Nature* (both with Kung Fu Treachery). You can listen to him read his work on Bandcamp and on LPs by the bands Theremonster and The Gotobeds.

Jan Ball has had 308 poems accepted or published in journals such as *Atlanta Review* and *Main Street Rag*, in England, Australia, Canada, Czechoslovakia, and India. Finishing Line Press published her two chapbooks plus her first full length poetry collection, *I Wanted To Dance With My Father*.

Roy Beckemeyer's latest poetry collection is *Mouth Brimming Over* (Blue Cedar, 2019). Previous books are *Stage Whispers* (Meadowlark, 2018), *Amanuensis Angel* (Spartan, 2018), and *Music I Once Could Dance To* (Coal City, 2014). Beckemeyer, from Wichita, is a retired engineer. One of his prose poems was selected for *Best Small Fictions 2019*.

Ace Boggess is author of four books of poetry, most recently *I Have Lost the Art of Dreaming It So* (Unsolicited, 2018), and *Ultra Deep Field* (Brick Road Poetry, 2017). His poetry has appeared in *North Dakota Quarterly, River Styx, cream city review*, and *American Literary Review*, among others. He received a fellowship from the West Virginia Commission on the Arts and spent five years in a West Virginia prison. He lives in Charleston, WV.

Gaylord Brewer is a professor at Middle Tennessee State U, where he founded and for more than 20 years edited the journal *Poems & Plays*. His most recent books are the cookbook-memoir *The Poet's Guide to Food, Drink, & Desire* (Stephen F. Austin, 2015) and a tenth collection of poetry, *The Feral Condition* (Negative Capability, 2018).

Rachel Bullock is a second-year MFA candidate in fiction at U of NH. Her work has previously been published in *Anasatmos* and *London Reader*. She is currently the fiction co-editor of *Barnstorm Journal*.

Eric Chiles had a career in newspapers, and now teaches English and journalism at a number of colleges in eastern Pennsylvania. His poetry has appeared in *The Auroean, Big Windows Review, Canary, Gravel, Main Street Rag, Rattle, Sport Literate, Tar River Poetry, Third Wednesday*, and elsewhere. His chapbook, *Caught in Between*, is available from Desert Willow.

Ellen Chia lives in Thailand and whilst pondering over the wonders and workings of her tiny universe finds herself succumb time after time to the act of poetry making. Her works have been published in *Ekphrastic Review, Nature-Writing, The Honest Ulsterman, Zingara Poetry Review,* and *Tiger Moth Review*.

Grant Clauser is an editor and teacher in Pennsylvania. He's the author of four poetry books, including *Reckless Constellations* and *The Magician's Handbook*. His poems have appeared in *American Poetry Review, Cortland Review, Painted Bride Quarterly, The Journal, Tar River Poetry,* and others.

Sandy Coomer is a poet, artist, Ironman athlete, and social entrepreneur from Nashville, TN. She is author of three poetry chapbooks and a full-length collection, *Available Light* (Iris Press). More than 150 pieces of Sandy's art have been published in literary arts magazines. She is a poetry mentor in the AWP Writer to Writer Mentorship Program and founding editor of the online poetry journal *Rockvale Review*. She is also founder and director of Rockvale Writers' Colony in College Grove, TN.

Robert Cooperman's latest collection is *Draft Board Blues* (FutureCycle). Forthcoming from Liquid Light Press is *Saved by the Dead* ("yeah, that Dead, the Grateful Dead, my lifelong obsession"), and from Aldrich Press, *Their Wars.*

Rachel Custer is author of *The Temple She Became* (Five Oaks, 2017). Her work is constantly informed by and wrestles with the values and struggles of the rural Rust Belt. Her Christian faith is vital to her understanding of the world and her art. She lives with her partner and their daughter in Northern Indiana.

Carl Miller Daniels has a new book due out soon – its title is *String Bean* and it is being published by BareBackPress. *String Bean* may already be out by the time you're reading this.

Matt Dennison, after a rather extended and varied second childhood in New Orleans, has had work appear in *Rattle, Bayou Magazine, Redivider, Natural Bridge, Spoon River Poetry Review,* and *Cider Press Review*, among others. He has also made short films with Michael Dickes, Swoon, Marie Craven, and Jutta Pryor.

David Denny is author of the short story collection, *The Gill Man in Purgatory,* as well as three poetry collections: *Man Overboard, Fool in the Attic,* and *Plebeian on the Front Porch*. Recent poems have appeared in *Carolina Quarterly, Spillway, San Pedro River Review,* and *Slipstream*, among others.

Timothy Dodd is from Mink Shoals, WV. His poetry has appeared in *The Literary Review, Modern Poetry Quarterly Review, Roanoke Review,* and elsewhere. His book of short stories, *Fissures, and Other Stories*, was recently published by Bottom Dog Press as a part of their Contemporary Appalachian Writing series.

John Dorsey lived for several years in Toledo, OH. He is author of several collections of poetry, including *Appalachian Frankenstein* (GTK, 2015), *Being the Fire* (Tangerine, 2016), *Shoot the Messenger* (Red Flag, 2017), and *Your Daughter's Country* (Blue Horse, 2019). He was winner of the 2019 Terri Award given out for best poem read at Poetry Rendezvous.

W.D. Ehrhart is a Marine Corps veteran of the Vietnam War, teaches history and English at the Haverford School in Pennsylvania. He is subject of *The Last Time I Dreamed About the War: Essays on the Life and Writing of W. D. Ehrhart*, Jean-Jacques Malo, ed. His newest collection is *Praying at the Altar* (Adastra, 2017).

Barbara Eknoian is a poet and novelist. Her poetry books and novels are available at Amazon. She lives in La Mirada, CA with son, daughter, three grandsons, and three dogs (which she never picked out). She's never lost her Jersey accent.

Kate Hanson Foster's first book of poems, *Mid Drift*, was published by Loom Press and was a finalist for the Massachusetts Center for the Book Award in 2011. She was awarded the NEA Parent Fellowship through the Vermont Studio Center in 2017. Her work has appeared or is forthcoming in *Birmingham Poetry Review*, The *Critical Flame, Comstock Review, Harpur Palate, Poet Lore, Salamander, Tupelo Quarterly*, and elsewhere. She lives in Groton, MA.

Andrea Fry is an oncology nurse in New York City. She published her first collection of poems, *The Bottle Diggers*, in May 2017 (Turning Point). Her poems have appeared or will appear in journals such as *Alaska Quarterly Review, Ars Medica, Barrow Street, Cimarron Review, Comstock Review, Graham House Review, J Journal, Plainsong, Reed Magazine, Stanford Literary Review*, and *St. Petersburg Review*.

Bill Gainer is a storyteller, a humorist, and award winning poet. His BA is from St. Mary's College and his MPA from USF. He is publisher of the PEN Award winning R.L. Crow Publications. Gainer is internationally published and known across the country for giving legendary fun-filled performances. His latest book is *The Mysterious Book of Old Man Poems.*

Alexis Garcia is currently an English graduate student at California State Polytechnic U, Pomona. While she hopes to become a community college professor, creative writing is her passion. When Alexis is not busy studying, she is writing stories, watering her plants, or rock climbing.

Tony Gloeggler is a life-long resident of NYC who has managed group homes for more than 40 years. His work has appeared in *Rattle, Poet Lore, New Ohio Review, 2 Bridges Review*. My full length books include *One Wish Left* (Pavement Saw, 2002), *The Last Lie* (NYQ, 2010), and *Until The Last Light Leaves* (NYQ, 2015).

Rosalind Goldsmith lives in Toronto and began writing short fiction four years ago. Since then, her stories have appeared in *Flash Fiction Magazine, Thrice Fiction, Litro UK, Popshot UK, Filling Station, Understory* and *anti-lang.*, among others. A new story will appear in *Burningword Journal*.

Jay Griswold graduated Colorado State U in 1979 with a masters degree in creative writing. He worked for many years as a ranger for the Colorado Division of parks, primarily on the water patrol. His books are *Meditations for the Year of the Horse* (Leaping Mountain, 1986), *The Landscape of Exile* (West End, 1993), and *Conquistador* (Main Street Rag, 2005).

Alan Harawitz is a retired NYC secondary school teacher; he's been living in a small town on Maine's southern coast for about 10 years. They "get lots of snow, lots of nature's bounty, cold weather, sweet birdsong every morning and gorgeous scenery (and very little traffic) – all of it contributing to the writing life." His first collection of poems was *The Day I Met Ava Gardner* (Deerbrook, 2019).

Wafa Al-Harbi is author of *the burning of the loaf* (Milad Publishing House) which was on the short list for the fourth session 2018-2019 Al-Multaqa Award for Arab Short Story.

James Croal Jackson has a chapbook, *The Frayed Edge of Memory* (Writing Knights, 2017), and poems in *Pacifica, Reservoir,* and *Rattle*. He edits *The Mantle*. Currently, he works in the film industry in Pittsburgh, PA.

Mike James' poems have appeared in numerous places throughout the country. Recent work has appeared, or is forthcoming, in *Iodine, Miller's Pond, Red River Review,* and *Negative Capability*. He's published seven books. The two most recent are *Past Due Notices: Poems 1991-2011* (Main Street Rag, 2012), and *Elegy in Reverse* (Aldrich, 2014).

Essam M. Al-Jassim lives in Hofuf, Saudi Arabia, and has a bachelor's degree in Education from King Faisal U. Work has been published in *Levitate* and *Fiction International* magazines. Other published pieces appeared in online literary sites, such as *Red Fez*.

Ted Jonathan was raised in the Bronx, he now lives in New Jersey. His books include *Bones & Jokes* (NYQ, 2009) and *Run* (NYQ, 2016).

Kendall Johnson writes and paints in Upland, CA, amidst ghosts of lemon trees and packing houses. He is author of *A Whole Lot'a Shakin': Midcentury Reconsidered, Fragments: An Archeology of Memory,* and *A Sublime and Tragic Dance* co-authored with John Brantingham. His collection of trauma and disaster stories, *Chaos and Ashes,* was scheduled for release summer 2020.

Gloria Keeley is a graduate of San Francisco State U with a BA and MA in Creative Writing. She collects old records and magazines. Her work has appeared in *Spoon River Poetry Review, Slipstream, Emerson Review,* and other journals.

Erren Geraud Kelly received his BA in English-Creative Writing from Louisiana State U in Baton Rouge. He loves to read and travel, having visited 45 states, Canada and Europe. The themes in his writings vary, but he has always had a soft spot for subjects and people who are not in the mainstream.

Casey Knott received an MFA in Creative Writing from Minnesota State U. She works in education, mentors students, tends to her urban farm, and helps edit *The Wax Paper*. Her latest book is *Ground Work* (Main Street Rag, 2018). Her poetry has appeared in a number of journals, including *Harpur Palate, Red Rock Review, White Pelican Review, Cold Mountain Review, Midwest Quarterly,* and *Poetry City, USA*.

Danuta E. Kosk-Kosicka lives in Maryland. She was invited to do the Stanislaw Lem translation on p. 9 for an anthology being prepared in celebration of Lem's 100th birthday in 2021.

Stanislaw Lem (1921-2006) was a Polish writer of science fiction and essays on philosophy, futurology, and literary criticism. Many of his science fiction stories include satire and humor. Lem's books have been translated into 41 languages and sold over 45 million copies.

Linda Lerner was born and educated in New York City. Her books include *Yes, the Ducks Were Real* and *Takes Guts and Years Sometimes: New and Collected Poems* (NYQ Books), and *Ding Dong the Bell* (Lummox, 2014).

Ellaraine Lockie is widely published and awarded as a poet, nonfiction book author and essayist. Her 14th chapbook is *Sex and Other Slapsticks* (Presa). Earlier collections have won Poetry Forum's Chapbook Contest Prize, San Gabriel Valley Poetry Festival Chapbook Competition, Encircle

Publications Chapbook Contest, Best Individual Poetry Collection Award from *Purple Patch* magazine in England, and *The Aurorean's* Chapbook Choice Award.

Anthony Lucero used to like it here, now he's not so sure. When he's not globetrotting, he can be found at Home Depot, his home away from home. The working title of his memoir is *Steam Sauna with Serial Killers*.

Tamara Madison is author of the chapbook *The Belly Remembers*, and two full-length volumes, *Wild Domestic* and *Moraine*, all published by Pearl. Her work has appeared in *Your Daily Poem, A Year of Being Here, Nerve Cowboy, Writer's Almanac, Sheila-Na-Gig,* and many others. She recently retired from teaching English and French in Los Angeles and is happy to finally get some sleep.

Jeremy Nathan Marks is based in London, Ontario. Recent poetry, fiction, and photography appears/is appearing in *Literary Orphans, Lethe Magazine, The Blue Nib, Bewildering Stories, Ottawa Arts Review, 365 Tomorrows, Unlikely Stories, Every Writer, As It Ought To Be, Writers Resist, Poetry Pacific, The Courtship of Winds, Bold + Italic,* and *Word Fountain.*

Michael Minassian is a contributing editor for *Verse-Virtual*, an online magazine. His chapbooks include poetry: *The Arboriculturist* (2010); *Chuncheon Journal* (2019); and photography: *Around the Bend* (2017).

Lisa-Marguerite Mora has won prizes for poetry and fiction and was nominated for Best of the Net and a Pushcart Prize. She has published nationally and internationally. Lisa offers workshops and literary services since 2002.

Linda Neal lives near the beach with her dog, Mantra. Her award-winning poetry has appeared in numerous journals including, *Jelly Bucket, Lummox, Prairie Schooner* and *Tampa Review*. She earned her MFA from Pacific U in 2019. Her first collection, *Dodge & Burn* (Bambaz) came out in 2014. Her next book, *Not About Dinosaurs*, will be out in 2020.

James B. Nicola's poetry and prose have appeared in the *Antioch, Southwest, Green Mountains,* and *Atlanta Reviews; Rattle;* and *Barrow Street*. His full-length collections (2014-2019) are *Manhattan Plaza, Stage to Page, Wind in the Cave, Out of Nothing: Poems of Art and Artists* and *Quickening: Poems from Before and Beyond*. His nonfiction book *Playing the Audience* won a *Choice* award.

William L. Norine studied law and music. He's been a professional jazz drummer and composer, a college music teacher, a Boston cab driver, a Wall Street lawyer, and served 10 years as a District Attorney. His poems have appeared in *Kansas Quarterly, Antioch Review, Lyric, Coe Review, GW Review, Aileron, Mankato Review, Midwest Poetry Review, William and Mary Review, Pacific Review Red Cedar, Amherst Review, Cape Rock, Candelabra (London), Karamu, Offerings, Poetry Motel, Poem, Willow Review, Cafe Review, Black Fly Review, Cornerstone, Touchstone, Ancient Paths*, and many others. He won *Nassau Review*'s 2005 Best Poem of the Year.

Kendra Nuttall has a bachelor's degree in English from Utah Valley U with an emphasis on creative writing. Her work has appeared in *Maudlin House*, among others. She currently lives in Utah, with her husband, David, and dog, Belle.

Suzanne O'Connell's recently published work can be found in *North American Review, Poet Lore, The Menacing Hedge, Steam Ticket, Typishly*, and *Forge*. O'Connell was awarded second place in the *Poetry Super Highway* poetry contest, 2019, and received Honorable Mention in the Steve Kowit Poetry Prize, 2019. Her two poetry collections are *A Prayer For Torn Stockings* and *What Luck* (Garden Oak).

Al Ortolani is manuscript editor for Woodley Press in Topeka, and has directed a memoir writing project for Vietnam veterans across Kansas in association with the Library of Congress and Humanities Kansas. He is a 2019 recipient of the Rattle Chapbook Series Award. After 43 years of teaching English in public schools, he lives a life without bells and fire drills in the Kansas City area.

Simon Perchik is an attorney whose poems have appeared in *Partisan Review, The Nation, Poetry, Osiris, The New Yorker* and elsewhere. His most recent collection is *Almost Rain* (River Otter, 2013).

Patty Dickson Pieczka's third book, *Beyond the Moon's White Claw* won the David Martinson Meadowhawk Prize from Red Dragonfly Press (2018). Her second book, *Painting the Egret's Echo*, won the Library of Poetry Book Award from *Bitter Oleander* (2012). She has won several contests for individual poems and has been in more than 50 journals.

Ian Powell-Palm is a writer, poet, and musician currently living in Bozeman, MT. He adores Ocean Vuong, Kendrick Lamar, and Allen Ginsberg. You can find out more about his poetry and his future readings at his Facebook page, *Powell-Palm Poetry*.

Puma Perl is a widely published poet and writer, as well as performer and producer. She's author of two chapbooks, *Ruby True* and *Belinda and Her Friends*, and three full-length poetry collections, *knuckle tattoos* and *Retrograde* (great weather for MEDIA), and her most recent collection *Birthdays Before and After* (Beyond Baroque, 2019).

Charles Rammelkamp is prose editor for BrickHouse Books in Baltimore and reviews editor for *Adirondack Review*. His chapbooks are *Jack Tar's Lady Parts* (Main Street Rag), and *Me and Sal Paradise*, (FutureCycle). Forthcoming are another chapbook, *Mortal Coil* (Clare Songbirds) and a full-length collection, *Catastroika* (Apprentice House).

Maree Reedman lives in Brisbane with one husband, two cockatiels, and five ukuleles. Her poetry has been published in *Unbroken, Rat's Ass Review, Grieve Anthologies, Hecate, StylusLit*, and won awards in the Ipswich Poetry Feast, including a mentorship with Carmen Leigh Keates. She likes to read and write poetry that has a story, in fact, she is a narrative addict.

Kevin Ridgeway is author of *Too Young to Know* (Stubborn Mule). Recent work has appeared in *Slipstream, Nerve Cowboy, Main Street Rag, Lummox, San Pedro River Review, Big Hammer, Misfit Magazine, Into the Void, Literary Orphans*, and *The American Journal of Poetry*, among others. He lives and writes in Long Beach, CA.

Brian Rihlmann was born in New Jersey and currently resides in Reno, NV. He writes free verse poetry, and has been published in *Blue Nib, American Journal of Poetry, Cajun Mutt Press, Rye Whiskey Review*, and others.

Edward Burke Roberts has been writing flash fiction since 2007. His absurdist tales, science satires, murder comedies, and essays have appeared online under his pseudonym "strannikov" at *Delicious Demon, Language Is a Virus, Gone Lawn Journal, Metazen, Dead Mule School of Southern Literature, Fictionaut,* and *The Miscreant.* He began writing verse in 2016.

Brad Rose was born and raised in LA and lives in Boston. He's author of *Pink X-Ray.* He has three forthcoming poetry books, *Momentary Turbulence* and *WordinEdgeWise* (Cervena Barva), and *de/tonations (*Nixes Mate). His story, "Desert Motel," appears in the anthology *Best Microfiction, 2019.*

Alex Z. Salinas lives in San Antonio, TX. He is author of *Warbles* (Hekate, 2019). His short fiction, poetry and op-eds have appeared in various print and digital publications, and he serves as poetry editor for the *San Antonio Review.*

Judith Skillman is recipient of awards from Academy of American Poets and Artist Trust. She is author of 18 collections of verse, most recently, *Came Home to Winter* (Deerbrook, 2019). Her work has appeared in *Poetry, The Midwest Quarterly, The Southern Review, Zyzzyva,* and other journals. Skillman is a faculty member at the Richard Hugo House in Seattle, WA.

Jared Smith's 14th book is *That's How It Is* (Spartan). His work has been published in hundreds of journals and anthologies in the U.S. and overseas, and he has served on the editorial boards of *The New York Quarterly, Home Planet News, The Pedestal Magazine,* and *Turtle Island Quarterly.* He lives in Colorado.

Jedediah Smith teaches literature, mythology, and composition at City College of San Francisco. Smith's recent work has appeared in *California Quarterly, Ekphrastic Review, Alba, Mojave River Review,* and *American Journal of Poetry.* He also edited *Parlando: Collected Poems of Ray Clark Dickson.*

David Spicer has poems in *Santa Clara Review, Delta Poetry Review, Reed Magazine, Synaeresis, Alcatraz, The HitchLit Review, Flatbush Review, Circle Show, The Phoenix, Ploughshares,* and elsewhere. He is the author of *Everybody Has a Story* and six chapbooks; his latest chapbook is *Tribe of Two* (Seven CirclePress).

William Taylor Jr. lives and writes in the Tenderloin neighborhood of San Francisco. He is author of numerous books of poetry, and a volume of fiction. He was a recipient of the 2013 Kathy Acker Award. He edited *Cockymoon: Selected Poems of Jack Micheline* (Zeitgeist, 2017). *From the Essential Handbook on Making it to the Next Whatever* is his latest collection of poetry.

Ron Terranova is a poet, short story writer, novelist and blogger from Huntington Beach. He is the author of the short story collection *October Light,* and his novel *I, Polyphemus* is now available on Amazon as an audio book. His edgy, provocative blog posts appear on rterranova.com.

Brian K. Turner has been featured reader at Hayward (CA) Art Council's annual spring presentation, and the John Muir Festival at Yosemite National Park. His work has appeared in *Blue Unicorn, Haight-Ashbury Literary Journal, Hiram Poetry Review, The Storyteller, Tiger's Eye,* and a host of other small, regional publications.

Martin Steingesser has published three books of poems, most recent, *Yellow Horses.* His poems have been published in *The Sun, The Progressive and*

Humanist, and many literary journals, including *Poetry East, Chautauqua Review, American Poetry Review* and *Hanging Loose.* He is Portland Maine's inaugural Poet Laureate 2007-09 and lives in Portland, ME.

Amirah Al Wassif is a freelance writer. She has written articles, novels, short stories poems, and songs. Five of her books were written in Arabic and many of her English works have been published in various cultural magazines. Amirah is passionate about producing literary works for children, teens and adults which represent cultures from around the world. Her latest book is *For Those Who Don't Know Chocolate* (Poetic Justice Books & Art, 2019).

Michael K. White wasted his youth as a member of the semi-legendary playwriting group Broken Gopher Ink. Their New York shows were *Human Skeletal Remains,* 1983, *A Fall of Stones,* 1988, *The Black Blood of Angels,* 1989, *Stigmata,* 1990, *Men In Black,* 1991, *The Amazing Melting Man,* 1991, *Confetti,* 1995, *Clazion Catches Light,* 1995, *My Heart and The Real World,* 1999-2001, and *Daguerreotype Dialogues* (written with Dianna Stark). His novels are *My Apartment* and *Change: The Numismatic Odyssey of a Quarter.*

Paula Yup returned to Spokane, WA after a dozen years in the Marshall Islands. In the past 40 years, she's published more than 200 poems in magazines and anthologies including those by Outrider Press. Her first book of poetry is *Making a Clean Space in the Sky.*

❧ *Patrons* ❧

Acme Lawn Sprinklers – L.A. Division
Big Al
Brenton Booth
Blue Horse Press
Alan Catlin
Favorite Sister
Roman Gladstone
David & Vicki Greisman
John Jacob
Max Mavis
Jeremy Michaels
Pandora
Reckless
Tish Rinehart
Rutabaga Rose
Glenn Sheldon
Jared Smith
Marc Swan
Ralph F. Voss
Zippy Zinger

(21) Anonymous

❧ *Special Thanks* ❧

Gerald Locklin
Putzina Press